THE VEILEI

Also Available from Valancourt Books

GASTON DE BLONDEVILLE (1826)
Ann Radcliffe
Edited by Frances A. Chiu

CLERMONT (1798)
Regina Maria Roche
Edited by Natalie Schroeder

THE ITALIAN (1797)
Ann Radcliffe
Edited by Allen W. Grove

THE CASTLE OF WOLFENBACH (1793)
Eliza Parsons
Edited by Diane Long Hoeveler

Forthcoming Titles

THE MONK (1796)
Matthew G. Lewis
Edited by Allen W. Grove

ZELUCO (1789)
John Moore
Edited by Pamela Perkins

COLLECTED GOTHIC DRAMAS
Joanna Baillie
Introduction by Christine Colón

THE ROMANCE OF THE FOREST (1791)
Ann Radcliffe
Edited by Caroline Webber

Gothic Classics

THE VEILED PICTURE

OR,

THE MYSTERIES OF GORGONO,

THE APPENNINE CASTLE OF SIGNOR ANDROSSI

A ROMANCE OF THE SIXTEENTH CENTURY.

Edited with an introduction and notes
by Jack G. Voller

> I think it is the weakness of mine eyes,
> That shapes this monstrous apparition.
> It comes upon me!
>
> JULIUS CAESAR.

VALANCOURT BOOKS
CHICAGO

The Veiled Picture; or, The Mysteries of Gorgono
Originally published by Thomas Tegg in 1802
First Valancourt Books edition, December 2006

Published by Valancourt Books
Chicago, Illinois
http://www.valancourtbooks.com

Library of Congress Cataloging-in-Publication Data

Radcliffe, Ann Ward, 1764-1823.
The veiled picture, or, The mysteries of Gorgono, the Appennine castle of Signor Androssi : a romance of the sixteenth century / edited by Jack G. Voller. -- 1st Valancourt Books ed.
p. cm. -- (Gothic Classics)
An abridgement of Radcliffe's Mysteries of Udolpho.
"Originally published by Thomas Tegg in 1802"--T.p. verso.
ISBN 0-9777841-8-5
1. Inheritance and succession--Fiction. 2. Guardian and ward--Fiction. 3. Young women--Fiction. 4. Orphans--Fiction. 5. Castles--Fiction. 6. Italy--Fiction. I. Radcliffe, Ann Ward, 1764-1823. Mysteries of Udolpho. II. Voller, Jack G. III. Title. IV. Title: Veiled picture. V. Title: Mysteries of Gorgono, the Appennine castle of Signor Androssi.
PR5202.V45 2006
823'.6--dc22

2006032781

10 9 8 7 6 5 4 3 2

CONTENTS

INTRODUCTION

You are holding an important book.

To be sure, it is not in and of itself a major achievement in literary excellence, nor does it break new cultural ground. If one were inclined to be uncharitable, it would be reasonable to say *The Veiled Picture* is a derivative piece of hackwork, lowbrow ephemera of no particular intrinsic merit.

So what allows, then, for any claim of "importance"?

In a word: *Udolpho.*

The Veiled Picture is, in a very real sense, a work of homage that acknowledges one of the single most important literary and cultural artifacts of the Gothic literary tradition and of the early Romantic period: Ann Radcliffe's *The Mysteries of Udolpho.* First published in 1794, and frequently reprinted, imitated, adapted, and plagiarized, *Udolpho* was the high-water mark of literary Gothicism and a substantial cultural achievement by any standard, and *The Veiled Picture,* by anonymously redacting that four-volume novel into an inexpensive, seventy-two page "Reader's Digest" version of the story, participated enthusiastically in a significant cultural phenomenon. And by this I mean not the phenomenon of the "bluebook" or "chapbook,"[1] those inexpensive and often sensationalized volumes that were a significant part of "popular" reading material in late eighteenth and early nineteenth century Britain, although certainly *The Veiled Picture* is just such a thing. No, what I mean is that *The Veiled Picture,* like all chapbooks and bluebooks, partakes of and documents a much larger Romantic-era cultural project, that of the "democratizing" of literary culture.

This democratizing is most famously associated with William Wordsworth and Samuel Taylor Coleridge's joint production of *Lyri-*

[1] Although I am following common usage by grouping the two sorts of texts together here, there is a difference. Chapbooks were largely a later eighteenth century phenomenon; small and short (anywhere from 8 to 24 pages), these inexpensive books were typically sold by itinerant peddlers, or "chapmen." Bluebooks such as *The Veiled Picture* were longer (usually running to either 36 or 72 pages), frequently featured a frontispiece illustration, and were commonly bound in blue paper covers. Bluebooks were published primarily between 1800 and 1820, in numbers that will probably never be known with any certainty. The Select Bibliography lists a number of excellent sources of additional information on chapbooks and bluebooks.

cal Ballads in 1798. As the American and French Revolutions sought to challenge the concentration of political and economic power in the hands of a ruling elite, Wordsworth, Coleridge, and others sought to wrest poetry from the grip of eighteenth century neoclassicism—largely the domain of university-educated urbanites—and make it something approaching a literature of and for the people. In later editions of *Lyrical Ballads* Wordsworth would expound his commitment to a poetics grounded in "a selection of language really used by men" and which took as its subject matter "incidents and situations from common life,"[1] thus making of poetry a record of ordinary life and personal experience, not of epic struggles and classical themes. The "new age" of poetry and other literary forms which the Romantic period inaugurated set the cultural stage for a broadening of literary subjects and possibilities. One of those was the Gothic, although for too long that term has been associated almost exclusively with a "high Gothic" that existed only in multi-volume novels such as those of Ann Radcliffe, Matthew Lewis, and Charles Maturin. In recent decades, however, scholars and historians have come to recognize the importance and vitality of other forms of the Gothic.

The meteoric popularity of the Gothic novel in the 1790s and the subsequent decade combined with increasing literacy to generate a significant body of Gothic literature in forms that maximized its accessibility both culturally and economically, most notably via magazine short fiction and bluebooks. There is no question that, particularly as concerns bluebooks, this accessibility comes with a price—*The Veiled Picture* is bereft of many of the finer features of its parent work—but for too long literary critics have focused solely on that price, dismissing chapbooks and bluebooks as sub-literary trash while overlooking a more diverse readership of these works and ignoring the fact there is much of cultural value in these texts, as Franz Potter has shown,[2] for such texts closely correlate to and in many respects re-enact more expensive, and more "substantive," Gothic productions.[3]

---

[1] William Wordsworth, "Preface to *Lyrical Ballads*," *The Poems*. Ed. John O. Hayden. (New Haven: Yale University Press, 1977), I, 869.

[2] *The History of Gothic Publishing, 1800-1835: Exhuming the Trade*. New York: Palgrave Macmillan, 2005. See especially Chapters 1 and 3.

[3] Angela Koch, "Gothic Bluebooks in the Princely Library of Corvey and Beyond," *Cardiff Corvey: Reading the Romantic Text* 9 (Dec. 2002). Online: Internet (4 September 2006): <http://www.cf.ac.uk/encap/corvey/articles/cc09_n01.html>.

The Veiled Picture is one of the best works to make the case for the significance of bluebooks, for it is a direct redaction—a compressed narrative summary, essentially—of one of the most influential novels of the Romantic period in British literature. *The Mysteries of Udolpho* typified and defined, in the minds of many critics and most ordinary readers of the time, the "Gothic craze" that so dominated popular (and even highbrow) culture in the 1790s and the opening decades of the 19th century.[1] Yet *Udolpho's* significance transcends any specific generic category. It is certainly a work that inspired many responses—Matthew Lewis's *The Monk*, most famously, to which Radcliffe's own *The Italian* was in turn a response—and many dozens if not hundreds of imitations and redactions,[2] including of course *The Veiled Picture*, but the popularity of Gothic fiction, of which *The Mysteries of Udolpho* may stand as representative, is a phenomenon much more complex than mere marketplace frenzy.

The key to that complexity may well lie in *Udolpho* itself. It is a novel, unquestionably, that some modern readers, and even some of Radcliffe's contemporaries, find to be overlong, melodramatic, improbable, clumsily constructed, and narratively uneven.[3] And if many of those flaws have to do with the expectations of modern readers, whose world is far from that of Radcliffe and her audience, it is also true that there is some justice in such criticism. While Radcliffe's literary talents are in many regards praiseworthy, the lasting cultural presence of *Udolpho* cannot be attributed solely to any "literary masterwork" status.

What made *Udolpho* hugely popular in its own time and important ever since is that it so effectively addresses the revolutionary and reactionary *zeitgeist* of Romantic-era Western culture. Although relegated for much of the later nineteenth and early twentieth centuries to a second-class status as a "genteel" work by a comfortably middle-class and traditional Englishwoman, *Udolpho* and its author have, in

---

[1] For contemporary reviews and reactions to Radcliffe and *Udolpho*, see Appendices B and C.

[2] See, for example, Appendix II, "Parodies and Imitations," in Deborah Rogers's *Ann Radcliffe: A Bio-Bibliography*, (Westport, CT: Greenwood, 1996), 181-190.

[3] See, for example, Terry Castle's introduction to the revised Oxford University Press edition of *Udolpho*, edited by Bonamy Dobrée (New York: Oxford University Press, 1998), ix-xix. At the same time, other scholars, such as Rictor Norton, argue that *Udolpho* "is one of the great works of European literature" (*Mistress of Udolpho: The Life of Ann Radcliffe* [Leicester: Leicester University Press, 1999], 97).

recent decades, undergone something of a makeover, a reconsideration of traditional understandings of the work and its creator. We are now able to see Radcliffe not as the mildly complacent affirmer of dominant modes of English politics and gentility but as a writer whose emergence from a background of non-traditional English religious and social thought (the "Dissenters," those English Christians who did not belong to the state-sanctioned Anglican church; specifically the Unitarians, in Radcliffe's case) validates a reading of her works as powerful cultural documents and affirms Radcliffe's own place, as Eugenia DeLamotte argues, in "the center of the Gothic tradition."[1]

As Rictor Norton has amply demonstrated, Radcliffe's mature thought was deeply conditioned by the liberal, even activist tendencies of Unitarianism in the late eighteenth century. While Anglican in practice, Radcliffe was profoundly influenced by the progressive ideas of the Unitarian connections of her family and its social network (including the famed Wedgewood family), and the relatively egalitarian and humanistic tendencies of her novels arise from this influence. Indeed, even one of the most prominent aspects of her novels, their "explained supernaturalism," can be attributed to the influence of rationalist Dissenting thought.[2] As a result of these intellectual and cultural influences, Radcliffe was equipped to recognize and engage the turbulent energies of her moment in a more adaptive and nuanced manner, to speak to them in a tone of something other than flat denial or cultural retreat, and this may be precisely what gave her work the vitality and the penetration to achieve its initial prominence and to remain highly visible even in a flood of post-Radcliffean Gothic hackwork.

What Radcliffe's most famous work may seek to achieve, and what may have been one of the elements to which so many readers (and publishers) were responding, is nothing less than the reconciliation of a fading past with a radically evolving present, one in which anxieties of personal identity and cultural stability are entwined—perhaps particularly for women—with emerging new political and economic realities. The political maelstrom of the French Revolution—at perhaps its most turbulent during the time Radcliffe was

---

[1] Eugenia DeLamotte, *The Perils of the Night: A Feminist Study of Nineteenth-Century Gothic* (New York: Oxford University Press, 1990), 10.

[2] See Chapter 6 of Norton's masterful biography, *Mistress of Udolpho*.

writing and publishing *Udolpho*—was only the most urgent of the revolutionary forces reshaping the Western world during the Romantic period in Britain. The recently concluded American Revolution had made political democracy one of the burning intellectual issues of the day, and the nascent Industrial Revolution was already reshaping the very landscape, as well as the demographics, the cultural milieu, and the economic and political structures of Britain. The literary revolution symbolized by Wordsworth and Coleridge was already underway. Radcliffe, neither a radical (although influenced by some of the same thinkers who were influential for various radical figures) nor a reactionary, may well have achieved, in her most culturally significant novel, a work that subsumes the literary and cultural past in a narrative form that offers its readers a path through the deep anxieties and extensive tumult of their time.

A detailed consideration of *Udolpho*'s narrative, intellectual, and aesthetic strategies is impossible here; it will have to suffice to say that Radcliffe's novel struck the resonant chord that it did by showing its readers a middle way, an informed if indirect recognition of the forces of upheaval at work in revolutionary Europe that resists them with a cultivated morality and understanding. Radcliffe's is a world in which the "given" is not a tool sufficient to the mediation of present turmoils; what is given—the tradition of sensibility and refinement and even of economic comfort—must be earned and "proofed"—not through the practice of trade or business, but through the willed cultivation of a morally informed and rationally bounded sensibility. Head and heart, virtue and passion, love and duty—all are tested in Radcliffe's novels, which consistently and emphatically recognize that personal success comes not through the rigidity of the one-dimensional, but through the development of a "rounded" psychology that balances conflicting impulses and guards against extremes either of indulgence or restraint.

In a time of violent political revolution in France and drastic reaction in England, a time of cultural and social change on a dramatic scale, Radcliffe's great accomplishment is her balancing act. *The Mysteries of Udolpho*, one scholar has recently suggested, is a Gothic novel that doesn't always seem to want to be Gothic,[1] but this may be looking at the work through the wrong end of our cultural telescope.

[1] Terry Castle, "Introduction," *The Mysteries of Udolpho*, ed. Bonamy Dobrée (New York: Oxford University Press, 1998), x-xii.

When we call it a Gothic novel, and then indict it for not living up to our expectations for that genre, we may be seeing the work through the sensationalism that sprang up so dramatically and lastingly in its wake, a sensationalism that seized upon the undeniably Gothic elements in the work (the decaying castle, the black veil, the persecuted heroine, the predatory males, the *banditti*, the midnight music, and so on) and pushed them to the foreground, making of *Udolpho* a flagship for a fleet—a veritable armada—that it never intended to lead. Indeed, this sort of "hijacking" of her work, and her reputation, may well have contributed to Radcliffe's withdrawal from literary activity and from the world in general, for post-*Udolpho* culture made her and her novel into something other than what they were.

The Veiled Picture is, it must be acknowledged, part of that post-*Udolpho* Gothic frenzy, and it is a work, like so many of those published in the wake of the popularity of Radcliffe, that has no interest in the subtleties that make *Udolpho* everything that it is. To read *The Veiled Picture* is not to read *Udolpho*. What is left out? While the plot of Radcliffe's novel survives intact—indeed, *The Veiled Picture* is a remarkably careful plot summary of *Udolpho*—the bluebook achieves that compression by dint of a ruthless trimming of Radcliffe's prose, eliminating description and metaphor, pruning Radcliffe's sentences and paragraphs to the bare, straightforward lineaments of plot.[1] The language has been radically simplified, made much more Anglo-Saxon, much less Latinate, less "flowery" and descriptive. Rhetorical subtlety and nuance are abandoned.

Also forsaken is Radcliffe's deep interest in the sublime and the picturesque, the compelling aesthetics of the Romantic period and ones which resonated so powerfully with her first readers. Scenes in which Emily's sensibility is revealed, and her cultivated and informed taste confirmed or extended, have been deleted. This purging of any real interest in aesthetics also eliminates the moral implications so aggressively linked, in the culture of the period, to aesthetic choice and preference. Perhaps this is because by 1802 the debate was so well-known that casual references were sufficient to indicate a character's innate goodness, or lack thereof; more likely, the intended audience of bluebooks was simply less interested in aesthetics and their ideological implications than they were in a sensational story.

[1] See Appendix A, "Compressing *Udolpho*," for discussion and illustration of the redacting of Radcliffe's novel into a bluebook.

And clearly the anonymous redactor of *The Veiled Picture* anticipated an audience interested only in action and swift progression of narrative, not in the nuances of moral edification, emotional refinement, landscape observation, or poetic reverie. This unquestionably changes the work severely, and certainly changes it in a direction contrary to that favored by most connoisseurs of literary achievement.

Why, then, read *The Veiled Picture*, this *Udolpho* in miniature? Well, aside from the fact it serves as a comprehensive précis of Radcliffe's novel, *The Veiled Picture* is not without its own charms. It has a brisk sense of action, an almost breakneck narrative pace that would later become one of the hallmarks of one of the last "Gothic" writers, William Harrison Ainsworth, who also recognized that new tastes—the tastes of a new reading audience—were coming into being, and Gothic bluebooks, far from being the nail in the coffin of a dying tradition, helped to create, and to nourish, that new taste. The more "refined" aspects of works such as *Udolpho* were edited out because, presumably, they were of little interest to many of the readers and purchasers of bluebooks, for whom gentility and "refinement" were often a cultural or social impossibility. Allusions to landscape painters would be lost on people without the means or inclination to visit museums or great houses; invocations of the sublime and the picturesque would be of little interest to people without access to the ongoing cultural debate about aesthetics. Not that all readers of bluebooks were at the bottom of the socio-economic ladder, by any means—Percy Bysshe Shelley was fond of them as a boy—but clearly the chapbook or bluebook was often targeted at a demographic that would be quite satisfied with a rapid narrative unencumbered by many aesthetic, cultural, or literary complexities.

What also is left, then, is a lot of fun, an entertaining narrative that grabs its readers and compels them through all of the highlights of one of the most famous books of its era. If you were even remotely in tune with popular culture in the Romantic period, you knew of Radcliffe and *Udolpho*. Despite the sensational title, which focuses on the single most iconic element in *Udolpho*, *The Veiled Picture* is not, unlike many other bluebooks, a "focused" distillation that concerns itself only with a single episode from a larger text. It is a complete redaction, one which retains every significant episode and character from Radcliffe's original.

As I mentioned earlier, to read *The Veiled Picture* is not to read *The Mysteries of Udolpho*, but it's the next best thing, and a delight in its own way. Enjoy.

Jack G. Voller
St. Louis, Missouri

September 26, 2006

ABOUT THE EDITOR

JACK G. VOLLER is the author of *The Supernatural Sublime* (1994) and co-editor, with Frederick Frank and Douglass H. Thomson, of *Gothic Writers: A Critical and Bibliographical Guide* (2001), as well as articles on the Gothic, cemetery iconology, and science fiction. He is Professor of English at Southern Illinois University in Edwardsville, where he teaches courses on British Romanticism as well as the Gothic and other forms of popular literary culture.

SELECT BIBLIOGRAPHY

The follow brief listing of scholarly works is limited to titles dealing with Ann Radcliffe, *The Mysteries of Udolpho,* or the phenomenon of the Gothic bluebook.

Castle, Terry. "Introduction." *The Mysteries of Udolpho.* Ann Radcliffe. Ed. Bonamy Dobrée. New York: Oxford University Press, 1998. vii-xxxiii.

Durant, David. "Ann Radcliffe and the Conservative Gothic." *Studies in English Literature* 22 (1982): 519-20.

Frank, Frederick S. "Ann Radcliffe (1764-1823)." *Gothic Writers: A Critical and Bibliographical Guide.* Ed. Douglass H. Thomson, Jack G. Voller, and Frederick S. Frank. Westport, CT: Greenwood, 2002. 349-360.

—. "Gothic Chapbooks, Bluebooks, and Short Stories in the Magazines." *Gothic Writers: A Critical and Bibliographical Guide.* Ed. Douglass H. Thomson, Jack G. Voller, and Frederick S. Frank. Westport, CT: Greenwood, 2002. 133-146.

—. "Gothic Gold: The Sadleir-Black Collection." *Studies in Eighteenth-Century Culture* 26 (1998): 287-312.

Graham, Kenneth W. "Emily's Demon-Lover: The Gothic Revolution and *The Mysteries of Udolpho.*" *Gothic Fictions: Prohibition/ Transgression.* New York: AMS, 1989. 163-171.

Haining, Peter. "Introduction." *The Shilling Shockers: Stories of Terror from the Gothic Bluebooks.* New York: St. Martin's, 1979: 13-19.

Howard, Jacqueline. "Introduction." *The Mysteries of Udolpho.* Ann Radcliffe. Ed. Jacqueline Howard. New York: Penguin, 2001. vii-xxxix.

Koch, Angela. "'The Absolute Horror of Horrors' Revised: A Bibliographical Checklist of Early-Nineteenth-Century Gothic Bluebooks." *Cardiff Corvey: Reading the Romantic Text* 9 (Dec. 2002). <http://www.cf.ac.uk/encap/corvey/articles/cc09_n03.html>.

—. "Gothic Bluebooks in the Princely Library of Corvey and Beyond." *Cardiff Corvey: Reading the Romantic Text* 9 (Dec. 2002): <http://www.cf.ac.uk/encap/corvey/articles/cc09_n01.html>.

London, April. "Ann Radcliffe in Context: Marking the Boundaries of *The Mysteries of Udolpho.*" *Eighteenth-Century Life* 10 (1986): 35-47.

Miles, Robert. *Ann Radcliffe: The Great Enchantress.* Manchester:

Manchester University Press, 1995.
—. "Ann Radcliffe (1764-1823)." *The Handbook to Gothic Literature*. Ed. Marie Mulvey-Roberts. New York: New York University Press, 1998. 181-188.

Morgan, Chris. "Radcliffe, Ann." *St. James Guide to Horror, Gothic, and Ghost Writers*. Ed. David Pringle. New York: St. James, 1998. 469-470.

Murray, E. B. *Ann Radcliffe*. New York: Twayne, 1972.

Napier, Elizabeth. "Ann Radcliffe." *British Novelists 1660-1800*. Dictionary of Literary Biography. Vol. 39. Ed. Martin Battestin. Detroit: Gale, 1985.

Norton, Rictor. *Mistress of Udolpho: The Life of Ann Radcliffe*. London: Leicester University Press, 1999.

Poovey, Mary. "Ideology in *The Mysteries of Udolpho*." *Criticism* 21 (1979): 307-30.

Potter, Franz. *The History of Gothic Publishing 1800-1835: Exhuming the Trade*. New York: Palgrave/Macmillan, 2005.

Rogers, Deborah. *Ann Radcliffe: A Bio-Bibliography*. Westport, CT: Greenwood, 1996.

—. *The Critical Response to Ann Radcliffe*. Westport, CT: Greenwood, 1994.

Satz, Martha. "Radcliffe, Ann." *British Women Writers: A Critical Reference Guide*. Ed. Janet Todd. New York: Continuum, 1989. 550-552.

Sedgwick, Eve Kosofsky. "The Character in the Veil: Imagery of the Surface in the Gothic Novel." *PMLA* 96 (1981): 255-270.

Swigart, Ford H. *A Study of the Imagery in the Gothic Romances of Ann Radcliffe*. New York: Arno, 1980.

Watt, William W. *Shilling Shockers of the Gothic School*. New York: Russell & Russell, 1967.

Wennerstrom, Courtney. "Cosmopolitan Bodies and Dissected Sexualities: Anatomical Mis-Stories in Ann Radcliffe's *Mysteries of Udolpho*." *European Romantic Review* 16, 2005: 193-207.

Whiting, Patricia. "Literal and Literary Representations of the Family in *The Mysteries of Udolpho*." *Eighteenth-Century Fiction* 8 (1996): 485-501.

NOTE ON THE TEXT

The Veiled Picture was first published in 1802 by the well-known and very active bluebook publisher Thomas Tegg, then published again in volume 2 of *The Marvellous Magazine and Compendium of Prodigies*. Such magazines were little more than collections of previously published bluebooks, and were quite common.

The text here follows that of the first edition. All editorial changes to and corrections of that text, such as of misspellings, omissions, or typographical errors, are noted either in the text in square brackets or in footnotes.

There is a substantial pagination error in the chapbook. The first page is unnumbered; the second page is numbered 76, and numbering continues through 96, at which point the numbering begins at 25 and continues sequentially to 72, the final page. (If the title page is counted as page one, 25 is the first accurate page number in the volume.) This is one of several indications of carelessness in the preparation and publication of this chapbook, a common occurrence in these works.

Character and Place Correspondences

(Characters are listed in order of appearance)

The Veiled Picture	*Mysteries of Udolpho*
Monsieur d'Orville	Monsieur St. Aubert
Emily d'Orville	Emily St. Aubert
Madame d'Orville	Madame St. Aubert
Monsieur Lebas	Monsieur Quesnel
Madame Lebas	Madame Quesnel
M. Caillot	M. Barreaux
Mme Tissot	Mme Cheron
Theresa	Theresa
Angereau	Valancourt
M. Moreau	M. Motteville
Lavoie	La Voisin
Marquis de Lormel	Marquis de Villeroi
Lisette	Agnes
Mignon	Manchon
Count de Plessis	Count de Duvarney
Signor Androssi	Montoni
Savilli	Cavigni
Mme Claron	Madame Clairval
Brandolo	Bertolini
Rodoni	Orsino
Valenza	Verezzi
Count Milenza	Count Morano
Signora Tessini	Signora Livona
Castle of Gorgono	Castle of Udolpho
Alise	Annette
Signora Mirandini	Signora Laurentini
Carolo	Carlo
Rovedo	Ludovico
Barbaro	Barnardine
La Fleur	DuPont
Count Amant	Count De Villefort
Alithea	Dorothée
Sister Doria	Sister Agnes

THE VEILED PICTURE

THE chateau of Monsieur d'Orville, in the year 1584,[1] stood on the pleasant banks of the Garonne, in the province of Gascony, commanding on the south a view of the majestic Pyrenees, and on the west the waters of the Bay Biscay. M. d'Orville delighted to wander on the margin of the Garonne, and listen to its gentle murmurs. He was a descendant from the younger branch of an illustrious family, and after the death of his father married an amiable woman, whose dowry added very little to his slender fortune. Some years after his marriage he retired to Gascony, the spot he had been attached to from his infancy. D'Orville felt a strong affection for every part of the old fabric, which his lady undertook to decorate with a chaste simplicity. The library occupied the west side of the chateau, joining to which was a well-stored green-house. D'Orville loved botany,[2] and often made excursions to the romantic spots around, with his wife and daughter. Adjoining to the green-house, on the eastern side of the building, was the apartment of Emily, containing her musical and drawing apparatus, in both which accomplishments she excelled.

The first interruption of happiness D'Orville had experienced was in the death of his two sons.[3] One daughter was now all his surviving care, who in person resembled her mother. Under her father's instruction she acquired a knowledge of Latin and English, that she

---

[1] *Udolpho* is set in the same year. While attempting to establish a veneer of chronological remoteness for the novel's action, the designation of these events as late sixteenth century is as superficial here as it is in Radcliffe's novel, a fact borne out by the novel's various anachronisms, several of which are preserved in the chapbook. The attitudes, thoughts, practices, and preferences of the characters all reflect the cultural reality of Ann Radcliffe's historical moment.

[2] Love of botany, or "botanizing" as it was known, was, in Radcliffe's time, another cultural marker of sophistication and sensibility, and enjoyed considerable popularity—and some controversy in that it acquainted young women with the "sexual" activity of plants.

[3] This information occurs much later in *Udolpho* (in Chapter 5 of Volume 1); here, it is likely introduced much earlier as a shortcut method of invoking readers' sympathy for D'Orville.

might relish the beauties of sublime poetry.[1] It was one of Emily's earliest pleasures to ramble, and her favorite walk was to a fishing-house of her father's, in a woody glen on the margin of a rivulet, that descended from the Pyrenees. This too was a favorite retreat of D'Orville's, to which he often brought his oboe, and played to the melting tones of Emily's voice. In one of her excursions hither, she observed a sonnet, addressed to the Nymph of the Shades, written in pencil on the wainscot. The lines were not inscribed to any person, and Emily could not apply them to herself, though she undoubtedly was the nymph of the shades.[2] She therefore, in vain, wished to trace the writer; the incident, however, was soon driven from her mind by the indisposition of her father, whose convalescence no sooner took place, than Madame D'Orville declined. The first scene he visited, when he had recovered his health, was the fishing grotto, accompanied by his wife and daughter, a basket of provisions, and Emily's lute. They spent the afternoon in wandering about the scenery of the place, leaving Emily sitting on the root of a fallen elm, reading a favorite author.—While she sat, her lute sounded in the grotto with a sweetness and execution that enchanted her. It presently after ceased, and she entered the fishing-house to discover the musician, but no one was there; her lute had been moved, and some lines added to those on the wainscot. While she mused, she heard a step without the building, and much alarmed, she caught up her lute, and hurried to her parents, who were sauntering in an adjoining glen.

In returning home, Madame D'Orville missed her bracelet, containing the picture of her daughter. She recollected to have left it on the table, when she went to dinner, and Emily ran back for it, but it was gone. This singular circumstance occupied their attention till they reached home, where they found Monsieur and Madame Lebas had just arrived; this gentleman was the only brother of Madame

---

[1] Ironically, this abridgement of *Udolpho* removes all of the "sublime poetry" which the original featured, not only in the poetic epigraphs (from Shakespeare, James Thomson, William Cowper and many others) which began every chapter but in the numerous poems which Radcliffe included in the text of her novel. Written by Radcliffe herself, these poems were always presented as the productions of her heroine and hero, and were intended as a potent marker of their cultivation, sensibility, and innate goodness.

[2] The first instance of a sentence-length plagiarism from *Udolpho*, although the original reads "was undoubtedly."

D'Orville, and had always disapproved of her marriage, as ill-suited to his ambition and her advantage. His own wife was an Italian heiress; in her disposition vain and frivolous. The conversation of Madame Lebas consisted only of the splendour of the scenes she had been involved in at Paris, when compared with the dullness of the chateau; to all which Emily listened with indifference. About twelve years ago Lebas had purchased of D'Orville the family estate at Paris, which the latter's father had left very much incumbered. The improvements he meant to make, and the noble company he intended to invite to his galas, occupied their conversation till bed-time; before, however, they separated for the night, M. Lebas requested a private audience with D'Orville, from which the latter returned much dejected. His wife could not penetrate into his melancholy, nor learn the subject of a second conference which took place the next morning; the guests dined at the chateau, and set out in the cool of the day for Epourville, lying about ten leagues distant, whither they pressingly invited the family of D'Orville, and then took leave. Emily returned with delight to that liberty their presence had restrained.

One evening, when D'Orville and his daughter had returned to the chateau from a romantic ramble, he found his wife had retired to her chamber very ill. The physician who was sent for decided that his patient had caught the fever, from which M. D'Orville had lately recovered. The malady increased, and in spite of the tenderness and prayers of a fond husband and child, it counteracted the power of medicine, and in a fortnight removed her from this transitory scene, leaving D'Orville, for a time, too devoid of comfort himself to bestow any on his daughter. Madame D'Orville was buried in the neighbouring village church, attended by a large train of mourners, after which the afflicted widower returned, and being alone with Emily, he tenderly kissed her, and bid her restrain the sorrow natural to such a loss. The first person who came to condole with the mourner was a M. Caillot, whose austerity, except on this occasion, would have induced a supposition, that he was divested of the finer feelings. He was followed by Madame Tissot, the only surviving sister of D'Orville, who had been some years a widow, and resided on her own estate near Thoulouse, whither she invited the relatives to pay her an early visit. But there were other calls which could not be dispensed with, and of this kind was a journey to Epourville, once his paternal domain.

Wishing to rouse Emily from her dejection, they set off for this great, ancient, and turreted chateau, surrounded with a large moat, and all the gloom of woody scenery.—On their arrival, they were led through the gothic hall[1] to a parlour, where sat Monsieur and Madame Lebas, who received them with a stately politeness, and seemed to have forgotten that they ever had a sister. After some general conversation, D'Orville requested to speak with M. Lebas, and Emily being left with Madame, soon learned that a large party was to dine that day at the chateau, of which Madame Tissot was to be one. D'Orville, when he understood this, would have departed immediately, but fearful the anger of Emily's uncle might, at some future time, injure her, he determined to stay. The party consisted of two Italian gentlemen, and several ladies, whose conversation was a melange of politics, and comments on Parisian fashions and the Opera. After dinner, D'Orville stole from the room to the old chesnut walk, which Lebas talked of cutting down.

D'Orville ordered his carriage at an early hour, and Emily observed that he appeared silent and dejected on the way home; but, supposing it might arise from the company and place he had quitted, she thought it would in a short time be removed. Week after week passed, however, and the oppression of his spirits and languor increasing, a physician was called in, who immediately prescribed the air of Provence, whither they prepared immediately to depart, having first discharged all the servants, except Theresa, to counterbalance the expences of their excursion. As the clock struck twelve, Emily had just finished packing up her books and instruments, when, in returning to her own room, she observed that of her father standing wide open. Curiosity prompted her to enter, which she did without her light, and saw him in an inner closet, turning over various papers and letters; he then knelt, and prayed most fervently; after this he

---

[1] "Gothic" in this sense refers exclusively to the architecture of the chateau. "Gothic" architecture, dominant from the twelfth to the sixteenth centuries in Europe, was characterized most notably by the pointed arch, but includes other features, such as piers, ribbed vaults, and buttresses, all of which become important load-bearing parts of the structure, thus allowing architects to reduce the "massiveness" of the building without sacrificing height or extent. See Appendix D, "Gothic Architecture/Gothic Fiction," for further discussion.

drew from a case a miniature picture of a lady,[1] which Emily could see was not that of her mother. This he pressed to his lips and heart with convulsive force, and at length returned it to the case, upon which Emily withdrew.

Every thing being ready, the travellers proceeded on their journey, after casting a lingering look at the chateau. The majestic Garonne wandered through the rich country they travelled in, winding its blue waves towards the Bay of Biscay. D'Orville now bent his way towards Roussillon, and soon after mid-day they reached the summit of one of these tremendous cliffs which overlook part of Gascony.[2] Here he spread part of a repast they had brought with them, during the time they partook of which, the tears often swelled into his eyes. Having learned that a hamlet lay near the valley at the bottom of the mountain, which they might reach before the evening set in, they bent their course thither through a craggy road, and arrived in safety. D'Orville now enquired of the driver the distance to the hamlet, but he could not tell, and all their resource was to travel on in the gloomy scene. They were at length roused by the sound of fire-arms, which was presently followed by a rustling among the brakes, and proved to be a handsome young huntsman, followed by a couple of dogs. The stranger offered to conduct them to the hamlet, which lay a short distance, and where he feared the travellers would be wretchedly accommodated.

When they reached the hamlet, there appeared to be no place fit to receive them; and the stranger and D'Orville said they would walk to the next village, Emily following slowly in the carriage.—On the way, D'Orville learned that his companion was not a resident in that part, but had only assumed the hunter's dress during the few weeks he meant to saunter away among its scenes.—D'Orville then enquired the road to Rousillon; and the stranger offered to conduct him to a village lying to the east, which immediately led there. The first object, however, was to get accommodated for the night in the village: they examined the various cabins of the peasantry, but they were so marked by poverty and want of room, that the stranger was

---

[1] The second use, in this chapbook and its source, of a portrait. See Introduction for further discussion.

[2] In the travel scenes of *Udolpho* not included in this chapbook, Radcliffe devotes considerable attention to the sublimity of the landscapes through which Emily and her father pass. See Appendix E on "The Sublime."

induced to insist upon D'Orville accepting his accommodations, which, though very humble, were much superior to any they had seen. On their way, they learned their friend's name was Angereau, who introduced them to his landlady; and, after supper, they were conducted to good beds, the only two in the place.—D'Orville was somewhat surprised to find in Angereau's room several volumes of the Latin poets, and his name, in the inside of the books, strengthened the high opinion he had imbibed of him from his conversation.[1] D'Orville rose at an early hour, much refreshed by sleep; and Angereau said he would accompany them on the road to Beaujeu, to where it divided, and D'Orville gladly accepted his offer, but could not persuade him to enter the carriage, as he preferred going on foot. As they went forward, Angereau often stopped to point out to them the peculiar objects of admiration around them; and when they came to the spot where the roads parted, Angereau took a lingering leave, and D'Orville observed he looked pensively at Emily. Not long after, putting his head out of the window, he saw Angereau standing upon a bank of the road, leaning on his pike, and following the carriage with his eyes. He then waved his hand to him, and Angereau, returning the salute, started away. Neither village nor hamlet appeared for many leagues, and the travellers again took their dinner in the open air, and then set forward for Beaujeu. Night had advanced, and the muleteer drove cautiously, when, on turning the angle of a mountain, they observed a large fire among the rocks, which led them to conclude they were some of the banditti[2] that infest the Pyrenees. A voice was now heard from behind, ordering the chaise to stop: in the next moment a man rode up to the carriage, ordering the driver to stand; when D'Orville, no longer doubting it was a robber, drew a pistol and fired. The man fell on his horse, and gave a groan, which induced D'Orville to jump out; when, to his astonishment, he observed it was Angereau, who now bled profusely from the wound he had received in his arm. Emily, on learning the dreadful catastrophe, fainted; and D'Orville, distressed between the two suffering

[1] That Angereau would take with him, on a hunting trip, volumes by classical Roman authors (in *Udolpho* he has works by Greek and Italian writers as well) testifies to the high quality of his education and to his taste.

[2] *Banditti* ("bandits") were robber gangs that preferred woods, mountains, or other secluded spots from which they would emerge to rob travellers. Reference to them was a Gothic cliché after Radcliffe.

objects, scarcely knew what he did.—Angereau seemed more concerned about Emily than his own wounds; and when he recovered, he assured her his hurt was but slight. They now applied a bandage to it, and placing Angereau in the vehicle, they slowly moved towards Beaujeu.—He had just explained to them, that, pleased with their conversation, he had determined to overtake and join them, when they came in sight of the fire which had blazed at a distance, and which, as they approached, was surrounded by gipsies, preparing their supper. Passing them without molestation, they soon after reached Beaujeu, where the wound was dressed, and declared to be dangerous. The travellers passed an agreeable evening; and the next morning, Angereau being very feverish and the wound painful, he was ordered to proceed no further. During the several days they remained there, D'Orville began to admire the unsophisticated and generous nature of Angereau; and, with pleasure, he said to himself, "this young man has never been at Paris."[1] They again travelled leisurely toward Rousillon, D'Orville sometimes amusing himself with botanizing, while Angereau and Emily were engaged in useful and refined conversation, in which they seemed to behold each other with mutual admiration.

The travellers now ascended some mountains of prodigious elevation, among which they loitered till they found it impossible to reach Montigny by sunset. Passing round a mountain, on the summit of which was an Alpine ridge, suspended as it were in the clouds, they continued travel on in their dangerous and craggy road, till they heard the vesper bell of a convent,[2] which Angereau proposed to go in search of. D'Orville said, they would accompany him, as he stood in need of refreshment and repose. Telling the driver to wait awhile in the road, D'Orville, supported by Angereau and Emily, followed

---

[1] Taken verbatim from *Udolpho*, this internal comment is a sign that Angereau / Valancourt possesses an uncorrupted "naturalness" and that his virtue has not been morally or emotionally compromised by time spent in an artificial and over-refined urban culture. Radcliffe's use of the phrase reflects the common Romantic belief in the integrity and superiority of the natural, an ideal that held that removal from the centers of civilization allowed the essential elements of humanity to develop in their true character, without being warped by the artificiality and pretense demanded by life in the increasingly impersonal and industrial urban centers of Western European nations. It is of course intentionally ironic that this sets up the later "corruption" of Angereau / Valancourt when his regiment is summoned to Paris.

[2] The vesper bell rings to announce the evening prayer, in older Catholic tradition.

the note of the bell, and entered a thick wood; on emerging from which, they saw the convent they so eagerly desired to reach. They knocked, and were admitted to the superior, who received them with courtesy, and granted their request. Angereau, with one of the friars, then returned to dispose of the muleteer, whom they lodged at a cottage skirting the wood. The travellers retired early to their respective apartments. Emily, occupied by the gloomy idea of her father's daily decline, lay two hours before she sank to sleep, which was interrupted by the chiming of a bell to summon the monks to prayers. After this she rested uninterrupted till the next morning, when D'Orville was sufficiently recovered to pursue his journey.—They often alighted from the carriage, and while D'Orville seated himself on a rude hillock to admire the scenery, he surveyed with pleasure the delight Angereau and Emily took in strolling and conversing together. It was near noon when they arrived at a piece of steep and dangerous road, which wound up an ascent, and, instead of following the carriage, they walked into a refreshing shade. Here they continued sauntering, till they found they had quite lost the road, and it became necessary to repair to a cottage at a little distance.

They found the cottager's wife in the deepest distress, seated with two strong beautiful children, who alternately looked up to their mother, bidding her not to weep.—D'Orville immediately enquired the cause, and learned that her husband was a shepherd, and a party of gipseys had stolen away his little all; and, what was worse, not only the few sheep, bought with the pittance they had saved, would go to his master, but he would be discharged for neglect! The value of the stolen sheep was considerable: D'Orville and Emily gave what they could spare, but Angereau supplied the deficiency, choosing rather to leave himself with only a louis[1] or two, than not restore happiness to the cottagers.—By the direction of the children, they were conducted through a by-path to the road, where they found the driver spent with bawling.—They continued their progress, on every side arising the majestic summits of the Pyrenees. Through a vast vista of the mountains appeared the low-lands of Roussillon, beyond which the waters of the Mediterranean shewed a distant sail

[1] A "louis" is a louis d'or ("golden Louis"), a gold coin first issued in 1640, and thus one of the anachronisms in this story, which begins in 1584. *Udolpho* features a number of such anachronisms, though most of them did not find their way into the chapbook.

steering along its misty bosom. Having taken a simple repast in the rude scenery, they descended the lower Alps, that bind Roussillon, and reached the plains, in which was situated the town of Aries, where they purposed to rest for the night. They met with simple but neat accommodation, and would have passed a happy evening, but for the gloom of separation. D'Orville intended to proceed along the shore of the Mediterranean to Languedoc, and Angereau, as he was perfectly recovered, to return home.—In the morning Angereau breakfasted with D'Orville and Emily, and the moment had arrived in which they were to part. D'Orville invited Angereau to La Vallée,[1] near which lived the elder brother of the latter, and who was not altogether unknown to D'Orville, who had conceived for Angereau a liking which made the regret of parting very keen.—They lingered at the door of the chaise several minutes after they were seated, and at length D'Orville pronounced the word farewell, which Emily passed to Angereau, and, after pressing her hand, they separated. A long silence ensued, till D'Orville observed, that when he was young he just thought and felt exactly like this young man; but now the world was fast closing upon him. Emily combated the latter idea, and D'Orville continued to please the ear of his daughter by speaking in praise of Angereau till they reached Colioure, where they dined, and immediately set forward for Perpignan, at which place letters were expected from M. Lebas. They arrived soon after sun-set, and found a packet for D'Orville, the contents of which so evidently and grievously affected him, that Emily was alarmed.—As they pursued their journey the following morning to Leucate, Emily pressed her father to state the cause of his unhappiness in such an interesting manner, that he consented, and told her, that when M. Lebas last visited him, he had stated, that a M. Moreau, in whose hands D'Orville's personal property lay invested, was in a state of ruin. "The letters now received," added D'Orville, "confirm the fact, by a statement from Moreau." "And must we quit our little estate at La Vallée?" asked Emily. "This," D'Orville replied, "depends on the state of Moreau's affairs." "Let us have but La Vallée," said Emily, "with myself to attend upon you,

[1] The name of the D'Orville estate—unlike the name of the castle—has remained unchanged from *Udolpho*.

and I covet no more.[1] In our minds we are rich, and with enough to supply the necessaries of life, I cannot be poor." D'Orville could not reply—he caught Emily to his bosom, and they mingled their tears together.

On the following day they recommenced their journey through Languedoc, and at evening reached a village, where they could not procure beds, as it was the time of vintage. There was no resource but travelling on to the next post, which the increasing illness of D'Orville rendered almost impossible.—Seeing a peasant walking on the road, Emily eagerly asked, if there were any house near where accommodation might be had? The man pointed to a turreted castle, almost hidden beneath some tall trees, which, he said was a strange place, and inhabited only by the steward and housekeeper. They immediately turned into the gloomy avenue leading to the chateau, and had not proceeded far, when a tall figure seemed slowly preceding the carriage. D'Orville called to the driver to bid him stop; but he declined this, saying perhaps he was some robber. In a moment after, he heard a deep hollow tone from some trees on the left;—it seemed to be scarcely human.—The terrified Michael[2] now turned his horses, not seeing any part of the chateau, and drove furiously down the avenue till he attained the high road, when they moved at a more moderate pace. "I am very ill," said D'Orville. "You are worse," said Emily, "and here is no assistance. What shall I do!"—At this juncture, the tones of a violin and tabor[3] sounded through a glen that bordered the road, and determined her immediately to proceed to the spot, leaving her father to the care of Michael. At the end of a long shadowy lane,[4] Emily discovered a party of vintagers merry-making, to whom she instantly unfolded her distress, and some of the elder ones accompanied her to the carriage. D'Orville asked, if he could obtain relief at the castle? but an elderly peasant assured

---

[1] In *Udolpho* Emily remarks that they shall retain only one servant; the change here, which imagines no servant other than Emily herself, would certainly be in keeping with the lower socio-economic-status readers who would be the likely buyers of a chapbook rather than an expensive four-volume novel.

[2] Michael—never properly introduced here—is a character whose name remains unchanged from *Udolpho*.

[3] A tabor is a small drum.

[4] See Appendix A, "Compressing Udolpho," for an illustration of how an extensive passage from Radcliffe has been reduced to a simple introductory clause.

him, it was unfit to receive him: but that his own bed and cottage were at his service. D'Orville gratefully accepted the kind offer, and was conducted in the vehicle to Lavoie's abode, who, as soon as they had entered, brought fruits, cream, and all the pastoral luxury his cottage afforded. D'Orville insisted upon Lavoie's sitting down with him, and soon drew the old man into conversation, by which he learned that his wife was dead, and he lived in the bosom of a numerous progeny, who were then merry-making. They had talked on this topic till the evening had set in, when, amidst the surrounding stillness, the sound of a guitar, exquisitely played, and accompanied by a melodious voice, softly stole upon their ear. D'Orville asked who was the minstrel, and was informed that no one could tell. "I often hear these divine sounds," said Lavoie, "but cannot learn from whom, or whence they proceed. They are seldom so early as this, and most commonly take their course to yonder chateau, the turret of which the moon now glitters on."—D'Orville asked the owner of the chateau's name. "The Marquis de Lormel," said Lavoie, "was once its owner, but he took a dislike to the place, and has not been there for many years. We have heard that he died about five weeks ago, and that the chateau has fallen into other hands." "Dead!" exclaimed D'Orville, with great emotion; "this is very extraordinary! But, pray, who has succeeded to the estates?" Lavoie said, that he did not recollect his lordship's name, but he resided at Paris chiefly, the chateau being left to the care of the steward and his wife, the housekeeper.

Lavoie had just drawn a heavy sigh from the bosom of D'Orville, by his affectionate sorrow for the fate of the late Marchioness de Lormel, when he started and cried,—"Hark! the music comes again! Listen to the voice!"—They heard the music gently approach, and then die away in a pathetic strain. Lavoie said, it was eighteen years since he had first heard these sounds, which his late wife and Father Dennis[1] had witnessed as well as himself, the latter of whom said, they were the warning strains preparatory to death. Emily heard this, and felt a superstitious dread steal over her as she surveyed the emaciated figure of her father, who asked if there was any convent near. On being informed, that that of St. Clair stood at no great distance on the sea shore, clouds of grief and horror overspread his countenance, and

---

[1] Another character whose name is essentially unchanged from *Udolpho*, where it is spelled (more appropriately for a Frenchman) "Denis."

he seemed as if struck with some sudden remembrance. When they had retired to rest, Emily leaned pensively on the little open casement, occupied in endeavouring to trace the cause of the extreme emotion her father had shewn at the mention of the Marquis de Lormel's death, and the fate of the Marchioness. Nothing, however, of sound, disturbed her meditation, from which she at length retired to her humble couch. Early the next morning the travellers arose, but little refreshed by sleep, and Emily observed her father so much altered for the worse, that she combated his proposal of journeying towards home till he was better.

He was of opinion that he was so much improved, as to be able to continue his progress, but the little exertion he made to keep up the spirits of Emily brought on a fainting fit; on recovering from which, he requested to be laid in the bed he had slept in the preceding night. Having summoned his daughter to his bedside, and bid her close the door, he addressed her thus: "My dear child, I would soften the painful truth I have to impart, nay, conceal it from you, but that it would be most cruel to deceive. You have observed how anxious I am to reach home, but you know my reasons for this: before I impart them, you must promise, solemnly swear to your dying father, to perform what he enjoins." Emily fell upon his neck, and vowed to execute his will, even at the loss of life and everlasting happiness. He proceeded: "I know my Emily too well to doubt that she would break her promise. Hear, then, what I am going to tell you.—The closet, which adjoins my chamber at La Vallée, has a sliding board in the floor, which you will know by a remarkable knot in the wood. By pressing one end, where a mark is drawn across, it will sink, and easily slide beneath the others. Below you will see a hollow place, in which are deposited a packet of papers. These papers you must burn; and I solemnly command you, *without inspecting them*. Under the board you will also find 200 Louis d'ors in a silk purse. But I have yet another promise to receive from you, which is, that you will *never*, whatever may be your future circumstances, *sell the chateau*, or give it from your own possession. I have told you, my child, how I am circumstanced with M. Moreau, at Paris. Alas! I leave you poor, but not quite destitute."

After this conversation, he appeared more at ease, and sunk into a kind of doze, from which he awakened quite resigned to his approaching dissolution. Having desired Lavoie might attend, he tenderly thanked him for the kindness he had received, and requested, that he would protect his daughter, till she was enabled to set out for Gascony. The good old man said he would do more, if D'Orville approved it: he would conduct her to the chateau himself, which the latter gladly accepted, blessing him for his paternal care. D'Orville next addressed his daughter on his consignment of her by will to the guardianship of Mad. Tissot, till she was of age, and his recommendation to her care afterwards. Having earnestly intreated Emily to cultivate her friendship, and received an assurance that she would religiously perform his injunctions, he fell back on the bed; then, uttering a blessing on her, and declaring that he died in peace, he closed his eyes, and in half an hour after expired without a sigh.

Emily was led from the chamber by Lavoie and his daughter Lisette, who exerted all their pious ability to comfort her. Not long after an invitation of condolence came from the Abbess of the convent of St. Clair, who had heard of D'Orville's death. After visiting the corpse of her father, and pressing his clay-cold hand, Emily retired to her little cabin, where, in her disturbed slumber, she saw him approach, accompanied with strains that seemed to descend from heaven. As they swelled louder, she awoke, but it was only to enjoy the reality, for now the music mentioned by Lavoie floated on the air, and charmed her to the window, where every object was lost in obscurity, and all was hushed, but the harmony that seemed to advance and remove towards the chateau. At last it entirely ceased, and Emily retired to rest.

The next morning another message came from the Abbess, and Emily, about an hour before sun-set, set out with Lavoie for the convent. The Abbess received her with a truly maternal affection, and her pious exhortation strongly fortified the mind of Emily to meet the approaching interment. Night had just set in before they commenced their return; they proceeded in the wood till Lavoie suddenly stopped, and said he had taken a wrong path, which led to the chateau, and at which Emily proposed they should enquire their way. Lavoie declined going near the chateau in the dark, urging, that the haunted music he had again heard last night was connected with it, to which he added, that there were many other circumstances belonging to the building, that he should never forget. A heavy sigh followed, and they soon regained the path to the cottage, where, after paying her last devotion to her father's corpse, retired to rest. The following day the body was interred in the convent of St. Clair, near the ancient tomb of the Lormels, according to the wish of D'Orville. After this event, Emily went to reside some days at the convent, where she lingered a few weeks under the influence of a slow fever, during which she wrote letters of what had transpired to Madame Tissot and the old housekeeper. The former soon after sent one of her servants to escort Emily to La Vallée, but gave her no invitation to come to Thoulouse; an incivility which Emily felt the more poignantly, from the recent death of her father.

On the evening before her departure, she went to the cottage to take leave of Lavoie, and make his family a return for their kindness. One painful scene yet awaited her, and this was to visit her father's tomb, to which she was conducted at night by one of the nuns. When the moment of her departure from the convent arrived, all her grief returned, and the Abbess assured her of an asylum at all times, and in all circumstances. She had travelled several leagues before she raised her eyes to survey the romantic scenery of the country. She slept that night at a town on the skirts of Languedoc, and the following evening drew near the chateau of La Vallée, at the gate of which she was met by Theresa, and Mignon, the spaniel, whose barking expressed the sincere joy he felt at his young mistress's return. Emily gave her hand to the old servant, and tried to restrain her grief, while she made some kind enquiries after her health. How silent and forsaken did the chateau now appear! the change brought a copious flood into her eyes, which gave relief to her mind, and enabled her to ask Theresa about the state of her father's old pensioners; some she learned were dead, and others recovered, and all who could were daily inquiring visitors at the gate. On entering her father's library, every thing spoke of him. The arm chair, and the book he had been reading, were exactly in the position he had left them. She seated herself before the desk, and looked over the page which he had read with so much delight to her. As she mused, she saw the door slowly open, and a rustling sound in a remote part of the room startled her. Through the dusk she thought she perceived something move; it then disappeared, and in the next instant she shrieked, perceiving it press beside her into the chair; her alarm, however, soon subsided, on perceiving it was her faithful dog.[1]

Having strolled round her father's favorite walks, Emily returned to the house, where Theresa had dressed a pheasant for her supper, which M. Caillot had sent, on hearing she was coming, with the kindest expressions of condolence. The heart of Emily was too full to relish any thing but sorrow, and she retired to her room. Letters, soon after Emily's return, were received from Madame Tissot, inviting her to Thoulouse, that she might act as her guardian. Emily, anxious to avoid the displeasure of her aunt, and yet unwilling to go, requested permission to remain at present at La Vallée, urging the necessity she had of rest and retirement. M. Caillot now paid Emily an early visit, and expressed himself in terms that endeared him to her. After several weeks her affliction began to soften into a placid melancholy. She ventured to touch the instrument D'Orville's fingers had pressed; to read the books he had delighted in, and to improve the education he had given her. Among her other rambles, she strayed with her lute to the fishing-house, which she had not entered since in company with her father and mother. Here every thing was just as they had left it. She had just seated herself, when a stranger opened the door, who stopped on perceiving her, and began to apologise for his intrusion. Emily thought the voice was familiar to her ear, but as it was dusk, she could not distinguish the features of the speaker, and therefore asked who was the intruder. "It is the voice of Mademoiselle D'Orville," said the stranger, meanwhile Emily advanced closer, and recognized the features of Angereau. He enquired after the health of her father, but tears choaked her utterance, and he learned the event of his death from the sorrow that followed. After he had mingled his regrets with hers, he led her from the fishing-house to the chateau, beguiling the way with an account of his return to Gascony. On the following day he said he was going to Estuviere, and, begging permission to take his leave of her in the morning, he retired.

Remembering the injunction of her father, Emily, on the next morning, ordered a fire to be lighted in the chamber where D'Orville used to sleep, and after breakfast went thither to burn the papers. Having fastened the door, she opened the closet where they were concealed, feeling an emotion of unusual awe at seeing the arm chair

---

[1] This incident, preserved intact from *Udolpho*, is a classic instance of the "animal-mistaken-for-ghost" trope common in 18h and 19th century Gothic-tradition literature.

and table, in which she had the last time seen him examining the papers with the greatest agitation. She readily found the recess in the floor, which contained every thing just as D'Orville had stated. The agitation of her mind as she fastened the sliding board, made her fancy, on turning round, that she saw his sacred figure sitting in the arm chair, and she sunk senseless on a seat. Returning reason soon overcame the illusion, and she took up the papers, though with so little recollection, that her eyes involuntarily settled on the writing of some loose sheets, and she was unconscious that she was transgressing her father's injunctions, till a sentence of dreadful import awakened her attention, and her memory together. So powerful was the influence of the words she had seen, that she hesitated for a few minutes to destroy them; but her high sense of duty overcame every other consideration, and she committed them to the flames, fearful that the only opportunity of explaining the dreadful sentence was passing away for ever.[1] On examining the purse, she found at the bottom a packet, containing the miniature of a most beautiful lady, the same she had seen her father weep over, and from the manner which he had spoken of the Marchioness de Lormel, she felt inclined to believe that this was her resemblance. Not long after Angereau entered, to bid farewell to Emily, and then entered into a recapitulation of the pleasant scenes he had lately enjoyed with D'Orville and his daughter, in wandering among the Pyrenees. The recollection of these views brought tears into the eyes of Emily, and Angereau changed the subject.

Before he quitted her, he pleaded for an acknowledgment, that he held a place in her esteem; and, after parrying the confession, Emily at length admitted he had even more. He then informed her, since he left the Pyrenees, he had been a constant lodger in the vicinity of the castle, wandering about its grounds, and constantly deferring, from delicacy, to present himself to her. Emily accompanied him to the plane tree, where her father delighted to sit, and Angereau, having kissed her hand, still held it in his, unwilling to depart. At this juncture Madame Tissot approached from behind the plane tree, and presented herself to the lovers. Angereau was immediately introduced

[1] The refusal to disclose here the words which Emily read is an early instance, in *Udolpho* and the chapbook, of Radcliffe's mastery of suspense-building technique, which achieves its most famous expression in her handling of the black veil scene.

by Emily, but the supercilious look of Madame made him instantly take leave, regarding the one with a glance of contempt, and the other with all the love he felt. When he was gone, her aunt enquired who that young man was and spoke so rudely upon the impropriety of admitting male visitors, that Emily answered, her aunt's neglect, in leaving her so long unprotected at La Vallée, was an invitation to the lover she now reprobated;[1] respecting whom, that she might be correctly informed, Emily entered into the growth of her father's esteem for him, and concluded by saying, that she should prefer staying at La Vallée to going to Thoulouse, since, where dispositions did not assimilate, unhappiness must ensue.

Madame Tissot, however, opposed her longer residence at La Vallée, and, on entering the chateau, bid her put up what she thought necessary, as she meant to return home the following day. The remainder of the day passed in the exercise of petty tyranny on the part of Madame, and at night, after giving Theresa orders at all times to hold the chateau in readiness to receive her, Emily wandered over the apartments, and round the gardens, filled with the idea of the parent who had made them dear, and which she feared she never should behold any more. She thought more than once she heard a footstep, and apprehensive it might be that of Angereau, she returned hastily to her chamber, and passed the remainder of the night in sleep. At an early hour the carriage was ready, and Emily, having, with many tears, taken leave of her old housekeeper, and obtained permission to take Mignon, the favorite dog of her father's, stepped into the vehicle with her aunt, and they commenced their silent journey.

Angereau, meanwhile, returned to Estuviere, his heart occupied with the image of Emily. He was the younger brother of the Count de Plessis, his senior by twenty years on whom his education had devolved when young. His little fortune had been much injured by the expence attending the cultivation of his mind, which was noble, impetuous, and a little removed out of the common track. He held a

---

[1] This indirect exchange between Emily and her guardian is one of the most "original" moments in *The Veiled Picture*. Radcliffe's Emily has far too much propriety and self-restraint to make any such remark as she makes here, although Radcliffe herself in this exchange (in Chapter X of Volume 1 of *Udolpho*) makes clear that Mme Cheron is indeed at fault in her failure to be a more concerned guardian. The redactor of the chapbook has converted an authorial aside into an indirect character remark, one quite inconsistent with Radcliffe's portrayal of her heroine.

post in the army, and had obtained leave of absence when he visited the Pyrenees, and became known to D'Orville. He now thought of introducing himself to the family of Emily, of whose flight from La Vallée, as well as their address, he was totally ignorant.—The travellers arrived safely at Thoulouse, and Emily was introduced to a splendid and glittering chateau, attended by servants in rich liveries. Till the entrance of supper, Madame Tissot entertained her niece with the grandeur of her own chateau, and the elegance of the company who visited it, which Emily listened to with a mortifying indifference. After supper she was conducted to her room, at a remote part of the chateau, accompanied by Mignon, who was now all she had to caress. Having invoked the protection and direction of heaven, she lay down to sleep, and rose early to ramble about the beautiful gardens of the chateau, for which her aunt the next morning at breakfast severely reproved her stating, as a reason, that she did not chuse to have any night visitors or garden assignations in her grounds. Hence Emily had no doubt, Madame had seen Angereau in the rounds on the night she slept at the chateau. She was informed that a large party was expected to dinner, and cautioned by Madame to divest herself of that diffidence which marked her ignorance, of the customs of high life. When the company arrived, Emily, in her mourning dress, became an interesting object to many of the visitors. Among whom were the two Italian gentlemen she had seen at M. Lebas's. Signor Androssi took the lead in conversation by the quickness of his perceptions, and his friend Savilli was as gay and insinuating as formerly,[1] and sometimes directed a tender look at Emily, who was sincerely glad when the day was over.

A fortnight passed in a round of dissipation and company in which Emily saw little pleasure, and felt much fatigue. Her happiest hours were passed in the pavilion of the chateau terrace, where she could indulge in the contemplation of the objects she esteemed. Having excused herself from visiting with her aunt, she repaired with her book and lute to this retreat; as she bent her looks towards La Vallée, she touched her lute with an expression of what she felt and reverted to an anxiety of knowing where and how Angereau had disposed of

[1] "Formerly": this clearly suggests the redactor of the chapbook has forgotten that he/she had edited out the introduction of Montoni/Androssi and Cavigni/Savilli earlier, which occurs in Chapter II of Volume 1 of *Udolpho*, shortly after the death of Emily's mother (page 21 in this edition of the chapbook).

himself. She was awakened from her musing by the sound of horses feet, and soon after saw by the twilight, a gentleman pass on horseback towards Thoulouse, so like the figure of Angereau, that she could not banish the idea from her mind. Madame Tissot returned home that evening with an asperity greater than usual, and on the following morning, summoning Emily into her presence, she held out a letter, and asked her if she knew the hand-writing, bidding her speak the truth. Emily looked at the writing, and declared she was unacquainted with it. Her aunt would not admit this to be the truth, and told her that she had requested her attendance to say, that she would not be troubled with receiving letters from a younger brother, who had no expectations,[1] and therefore required Emily to neither see nor write to him without her consent. This she readily gave, and then was permitted to retire, which she did, to her favorite pavilion, where she canvassed over her former behaviour to Angereau, and saw nothing to censure in it.

While she was weighing the hard task of resigning up one, who had interested her heart by his apparent virtues, Angereau opened the door of the pavilion, and entered.—It was difficult to say which predominated most in the mind of Emily, joy at meeting her lover, or terror at her aunt's displeasure, should she hear of this meeting. Angereau had just stated that his object was to present himself to her family, when Madame Tissot turned into the avenue, as they were quitting the pavilion to return to the chateau. Emily advanced with Angereau to meet her, and receiving a look of indignation from her aunt, she retired, leaving them together. Not long after Madame returned, saying that she had put an end, by her decided conduct, to the whole affair; adding, that her brother had left her a troublesome office; but, if she found the intimacy renewed, a convent would be the alternative. He had confessed himself a poor younger brother, dependent only on his post in the army for support, and vowed, that he would receive his dismissal only from the lips of Emily; which Madame declared she would take means to prevent. Emily rejoiced at the frankness of his confession, and pointed out to her aunt the generosity of his conduct. Madame now required Emily to dress, and

---

[1] As a younger brother, Angereau / Valancourt would not, according to the English legal principle of primogeniture ("first-born"), be able to inherit family property, which under most circumstances would pass intact to the eldest son.

attend her to the house of Madame Claron, an elderly widow lady, who had lately quitted Paris for Thoulouse, and lived on an estate of her late husband's. The magnificence of her entertainments much excelled those of Madame Tissot, who was flattered by being admitted among the number of her friends. The entertainments of the evening consisted of a ball and supper, *al fresco*.[1] Emily surveyed the fantastic scene with a melancholy pleasure, till, among the groups of dancers, she perceived Angereau, standing near a beautiful young lady, with whom he conversed in the most familiar and attentive manner. The Count Beauvilliers[2] had engaged Emily so closely in conversation, that she could not retire, either to hide her uneasiness, or prevent her eyes from meeting those of Angereau, whose looks expressed an equal mortification with her own.

Emily would have withdrawn, but this would too plainly have spoken the interest he held in her heart; she therefore continued conversing with the Count, whose remarks soon fell upon Angereau and his partner. "That lady," said he, "is ranked among the beauties and fortunes of Thoulouse: the young chevalier who dances with her seems to be accomplished in every thing but dancing; he either is very neglectful or very ignorant."—Shortly after the Chevalier Angereau came towards them, bowed low to Madame Tissot, and then, with an earnest dejected look at Emily, he turned aside, as her aunt was with her.—Signor[3] Savilli now joining them, a conversation ensued upon the company, in which Mad. Tissot seemed chagrined that Signor Androssi had not paid her his respects: his friend made an apology for him, but it was ill received; and the jealous manner of Emily's aunt suggested to her, that she wished to receive the addresses of the accomplished Androssi, who soon after joined the party, and expressed his sorrow at being so long absent; but Mad. Tissot, to let him see her disappointment, addressed her conversation only to

[1] "al fresco": outside (Italian, "in the fresh [air]"). While Radcliffe presents this ball as occurring outside, she takes the trouble to note that it is a "fancy ball," which would have required formal clothing, typically representing a fictional or historical character. This upper-class aspect of the ball has been eliminated for the chapbook.

[2] One of the few higher-class characters whose name has remained more-or-less unchanged from the original, where Radcliffe denotes him as "Count Bauvillers." Somewhat surprisingly, the chapbook version of this name is better French.

[3] In an obvious typesetting or proofreading error, Savilli is here identified in the chapbook as "Signora Savilli."

Savilli. The supper was served in different pavilions in the gardens, and in the saloon,[1] where chance placed Angereau at the same table with Mad. Tissot and Emily. He was at the bottom, and therefore did not perceive Emily, who sat at some distance from him, and could not help glancing at the attention he paid to his partner, who was the beautiful Mademoiselle D'Emery, of a very large fortune, and much accomplished. Madame Tissot singled out Angereau as the object of her contempt and ridicule, and next arraigned the taste and discrimination of Mad. Claron, in suffering a person of no condition nor family to be admitted to her parties. "I perceive," said a lady, who sat near Mad. Tissot, "that the person you have been speaking of is Mad. Claron's nephew."—"Impossible!" cried Mad. Tissot, and she now changed from the most unmerited censure to the most extravagant praise. During the remainder of the supper, and after, the embarrassment of Mad. Tissot, though she strove to conceal it, was visible to every one, and it was with pleasure Emily heard her propose to return home. Signor Androssi handed her to her carriage, and Savilli followed with Emily. On reaching the chateau, they separated for the night; and, on the following morning, as Emily sat at breakfast with her aunt, a letter was brought her from Angereau, which Emily immediately placed in her aunt's hand, who returned it, bidding her read the contents, which stated that he would receive his dismission from Emily only. "We must see the young man," said Mad. Tissot, "and I will write him a note to that purpose." In consequence of this he shortly after came, and was received in a different manner to what he had hitherto experienced. She regretted that he had not mentioned he was nephew to Mad. Claron, which would have been a sufficient introduction to her house, and on the strength of which he might continue his visits to Emily, but enjoined him never to think of marrying till he had risen in his profession, and she thought it was proper; adding, that, as she was Emily's guardian, her charge had no choice of action but her's. The lovers bowed assent, and inwardly hoped that fortune would do more towards their happiness than the self-interested and ambitious views of Mad. Tissot.

Angereau made frequent visits to Emily, and she passed in his society the happiest hours she had known since the death of her fa-

[1] "Saloon" (the same word is used in *Udolpho*) is a variant spelling of "salon," a formal room used for the reception of guests.

ther; while her aunt increased her intercourse with Mad. Claron, for the pleasure of announcing the attachment that subsisted between their nephew and niece. The regiment of Angereau lay near Toulouse,[1] and thus he was enabled to pass the winter months in peace and pleasure with Emily. The éclat[2] to which this splendor of Mad. Claron's entertainments had raised her name, now had a powerful operation on the mind of Mad. Tissot to unite the two families by a hymeneal union,[3] and she proposed to advance, on the side of Emily, a sum equal to Mad. Claron's liberality to her nephew. This was directly agreed upon, announced to the lovers, and preparations for the nuptials were ordered to [be] made. During this, Androssi became the acknowledged lover of Mad. Tissot, and his visits were incessant. Neither Emily nor Angereau had ever liked this Italian, and they much disapproved the unequal courtship, in point of age and other circumstances, between Mad. Tissot and Androssi. The former, one morning, sent for Emily, and, to her surprise, told her that henceforth she must consider Signor Androssi as her uncle, to whom she had been married on the preceding morning[4] privately; and that she meant to give a splendid entertainment on the occasion, at which she should expect the company of Angereau and herself, whose nuptials would, from this circumstance, be a little delayed. The new husband having taken possession of the chateau, within a few days after the promised magnificent supper and ball was given, at which Mad. Claron excused herself from attending.[5] Angereau was Emily's partner; and Madame Androssi talked and danced incessantly, while her husband appeared silent and haughty, seemingly weary of the parade, and frivolous company it had brought together. A few weeks had only elapsed, when Madame Androssi told Emily she was to ac-

---

[1] Another typesetting or proofreading error: everywhere else in *The Veiled Picture* the name of this city is spelled "Tholouse," following Radcliffe's practice.

[2] Éclat (the word is not used in Radcliffe) means "public exposure" or "notoriety."

[3] That is, a marriage (Hymen was the Greek god of marriage); Radcliffe's corresponding passage uses the simple phrase "immediate marriage," suggesting a sudden urge, on the part of the redactor, to heighten the tone of the chapbook, at least in this passage. The use of "incessant" two sentences further on may also be part of an indulgence in a more polysyllabic vocabulary, though it is not a particularly felicitous choice. Radcliffe merely refers to the "increasing frequency" of Montoni's visits.

[4] In *Udolpho*, Emily is informed of her aunt's marriage the same day.

[5] An awkward sentence fragment—more evidence, it is likely, of haste or carelessness in the production of *The Veiled Picture*.

company them to Venice, where her husband had a fine mansion, and that the proposed connection between her and Angereau must for the future be wholly abandoned, since her husband had ordered it so for his niece's advancement.—Emily was so overcome by this sudden reverse of her fondest hopes, that she retired to her apartment, and wept till her tears were exhausted. When she was summoned to dinner, Androssi was absent, nor could his wife, whose jealousy was alarmed, account for the seeming neglect.

In retiring from dinner across the hall, Emily met Angereau, who had just entered. He was surprised to see her in tears, and, requesting a few minutes conversation, led her to the open door of an apartment.—He had no sooner heard what had passed between Emily and her aunt, than his indignation rose against Androssi, and it was only at Emily's earnest entreaty, he agreed to drop the prospect of personal revenge. She comforted his despondency with the assurances of her love, and the reflection, that in little more than a year she should be of age, and out of the power of her capricious tyrannical relations. Having taken a tender adieu of Emily, he, on his return home, wrote to Androssi, requesting an interview, which the latter refused as of no utility. Several letters passed without any farther success, till at last those of Angereau were returned unopened; upon which the latter flew to the chateau, but was denied admittance. In the mean time, Androssi hastened the preparations for his journey; and the last day of Emily's stay at Thoulouse arrived without affording a line of comfort to Angereau who had twice written to Emily, proposing a clandestine marriage, but which reached only the hand of her guardian. Madame Claron took no active steps to renew the match which Androssi had broken off. She had never esteemed Mad. Tissot, and now thought that her nephew's interest would be better consulted in either delaying his marriage, or uniting into a better family. At length the last night arrived of Emily's being in the same town with Angereau: the consideration that she had perhaps seen him for the last time made her faint, and she went to the window of her chamber to inhale the reviving air. The moon-light and stillness that overspread the scene induced her to take a walk in the garden, and, silently descending the stairs to the great hall, she opened the door, and entered the avenue. Having traversed the walks which served to bring Angereau to her more immediate fancy, she took her seat in the pavilion, and in a moment found herself in the embraces of the man she most esteemed on earth. "My Emily," said he, "I have haunted these gardens every night, and heaven has at last blessed me with an opportunity of cancelling my despair!" She uttered vows of unceasing love and constancy; and Angereau ventured to propose a clandestine marriage on the following morning at the church of the Augustines. The conflict which the mind of Emily now suffered between love and duty, overcame the strength of her faculties, and she fainted in his arms. When she recovered, she told him all the reasons why she rejected his proposal, and was about to retire to the castle, when Angereau conjured her to attend to some particulars which he would not mention before, that her decision upon his proposal might be the more uninfluenced. As they walked upon the terrace, he proceeded as follows:—"Little doubt exists that this Androssi is of Madame Lebas's family, but that he is a man of real fortune appears very doubtful, from some information I gathered by accident from an Italian who did not know I was acquainted [with] him. He said, that Androssi was considered abroad as a man of desperate fortune and character, and that he had a castle, situated among the Appennines, of which some strange stories are told. My eagerness to learn further particulars putting my informant on his guard, I could learn nothing more of him, though it appeared to me that he had much to disclose.—Think then, Emily, what I must feel to know you are placed in the absolute power of such a doubtful character as Androssi."—Emily seemed awhile absorbed in thought, but she did not change her resolution. As the love of Angereau magnified her danger, she combated the folly of believing reports which even did not identify that Androssi was the person so alarmingly spoken of.—Angereau finding it in vain to remove her resolution, pressed her to his heart, and held her there in silence, weeping. Having once more tenderly consigned each other to the protection of heaven, Angereau tore himself from the spot, and Emily hurried from the avenue to her chamber to seek repose.[1]

The carriages and baggage being ready at an early hour, the family of Androssi commenced their journey, Emily riding in the second carriage with Madame Androssi's woman, Alise. They stopped on their way to take up Signor Savilli, and soon reached a village, at

[1] This marks the end of Volume I of Udolpho.

which they changed horses. During several days the travellers journeyed over the plains of Languedoc, and then traversing Dauphiny, they began to ascend the Alps, where such scenes of sublimity rose to astonish the eye, that, for a time, they abstracted the attention of Emily from Angereau. With what delight did she view the setting sun, which the lovers had previously agreed to look up to at a certain hour, pleased with the idea of having a common object of interest between them!—The snow had not yet melted on the summit of Mount Cenis, over which the party passed, and then descended on the Italian side to the grassy vales of Piedmont; beyond lay the plains of Lombardy and the city of Turin. Passing Novalesa, they reached the small ancient town of Susa, which formerly guarded the pass of the Alps into Piedmont. Here they rested for the night at an inn, and, during supper, Emily first caught a strain of Italian music. The long-drawn tones of a violin, playing an adagio air, stole so impressively upon her ear, that it drew to her memory the music which had enchanted her at a former period. Savilli smiled at the surprise of Emily, and remarked the performer was one of the inn-keeper's family, and such exquisite music was very common among the peasantry.—Having retired for a few hours to rest they recommenced their journey at an early hour, as Androssi meant to dine at Turin. As they approached that city the magnificence of the stupendous Alps in the background became visible; to the east stretched the plains of Lombardy, and beyond the towers of Turin lay the Appennines bounding the horizon. Androssi, who had been often at Turin, did not care about indulging his wife's request to view the palace, but ordered dinner, and then departed for Venice. His manners during the journey were very reserved to his wife, and Emily observed, that when Savilli mentioned any daring exploit, of which the convulsed state of the country then furnished many, the eye of Androssi glowed with a lustre that partook more of the glare of malice than the brightness of valour.—On entering the Milanese, the gentlemen assumed the Italian dress, and Androssi added to his hat the military plume, which Emily imagined he wore to pass only with the more security through the parties of soldiers which overran the country.—Though the devastations of war were every where visible, they reached Milan in safety, and passed on to Verona. In their way they encountered the army of the victorious Ubaldo, who was returning with the spoils he had won into his own principality. This commander was a friend of Androssi's, and he drew up on the road side to give the army the pass, and welcome the haughty chief, who invited him to be present at a grand triumphant fete he meant to give the following day.—This Androssi declined, and taking a farewell of the General, they proceeded to Verona, which town they slept at, and set off the next day for Padua, whence they embarked on the Brenta for Venice.

Nothing could exceed Emily's admiration on her first view of this magnificent assemblage of islets, palaces and towers. It was Carnival time,[1] and the fantastic amusements extended along the whole line of those enchanting shores. Their barge passed on, amidst floating orchestras of music, to the grand canal, where Androzzi's mansion was situated. It stopped at the portico of a large house, from whence a servant of Androssi's crossed the terrace, and immediately the party disembarked. From the portico they passed a noble hall to a staircase of marble, which led to a saloon fitted up in a style of eastern magnificence. Soon after their arrival, Androssi ordered his gondola, and went out with Savilli to mingle in the scenes of the evening. Emily, placing herself at the lattice of her window, enjoyed the festivity exhibited in the dancing girls and singing groupes which succeeded one another, while Madame Androssi remained sullenly within. Moving now to the balcony, and putting on her veil, she saw a beautiful procession of gondolas, accompanied by the fabled deities of the city, Neptune, and Venice, personified as his queen, who seemed to float to the sweetest sounds on the water. From this beautiful spectacle she was called to supper, to which Androssi did not return. When Emily was conducted to her chamber, she passed through long suites of noble rooms, which, from their desolate aspect, seemed not to have been occupied for many years. Her lattice commanded an extensive view of the Adriatic, contemplating which for a time, and heaving a sigh to Angereau, she sunk to rest. Androssi, whose delight lay in the energetic passions and tempests of life, had spent the night in gaming with Savilli and a party of young men, who had more money than virtue or rank. Some of these he respected for superior play and ability, particularly three, the Signors Brandolo, Rodoni, and Valenza. The first was gay, extravagant, and generously brave: the second

[1] Carnival was the period of revelry prior to Lent, ending on Shrove Tuesday (or Mardi Gras).

was the favourite of Androssi; he was artful, cruel, and malignant: the last was daring, selfish, wavering, and easily swayed. Such were the companions whom Androssi invited to his table the nest day; to whom must be added Count Milenza, and a Signora Tessini, a lady of distinguished merit. Madame Androssi appeared reserved; she disliked her husband's companions, and shewed her attention only to the Count Milenza, while Emily found the person and manners of Signora Tessini had won her involuntary regard. In the cool of the evening the party embarked in Androssi's gondola, and rowed out upon the sea. The distant music, skimming on the water from other gondolas, inspired Androssi[1] with sympathetic emotions, and snatching up Emily's lute, he played and sung in the most finished style a little plaintive air, the words of which he addressed to Emily, and then returned the instrument to her with a deep sigh. Emily followed next, and performed a slow movement and a lively air, the latter of which was encored. The rest of the company alternately sung or played, till Androssi expressed a desire to return, which was opposed by the Count. A boat now passing by, Androssi pleaded business for his absence, and, with his friend, Rodoni, departed to visit the gaming-house. The Count having secretly dispatched a servant in Androssi's boat for his own gondola, it soon after came, and the whole party removed into it: while they partook of a collation of fruit and wines,[2] the band of music followed in another gondola, playing to the movement of the oars in sweetest harmony.

During this, the compliments and behaviour of the Count were so pointed to Emily, that she assumed a mild reserve, and directed her conversation to Signora Tessini. Emily now wished they were on shore again; but it was near midnight before the gondolas approached St. Mark's palace, after which they adjourned to supper at the elegant castle of the Count. Before they separated, he invited Madame Androssi and her party to take coffee in his box at the opera the following evening, which was accepted. After this they were escorted home, whither Androssi returned late in the morning, in a very ill humour, having lost considerably at play. Several ladies vis-

---

[1] In what is surely a redactor's error, here Androssi/Montoni takes up the lute and performs, although everywhere else in the novel he is depicted as a man with little interest in music. In *Udolpho* it is the Count who seizes the lute and plays.

[2] "Fruits and ice" in *Udolpho*.

ited them the next day, among whom a Signora Angela[1] attracted Emily's regard and attention. At night they adjourned to the opera with the Count, where the only feeling excited in her mind was the inferiority of art to the sublimity of nature. Several weeks passed in the course of customary visits, during which the Count took every opportunity of persecuting Emily with his visits.

Not long after Androssi's arrival at Venice, he had received a packet from M. Lebas, stating, that he was coming to take possession of an estate on the Brenta, devolved to him by the death of his wife's uncle, the brother of Lebas' late mother, to whom Androssi was related by the father's side. Though Androssi had no claim to these possessions, he could ill conceal the envy which Lebas' letter excited. The indifference of Androssi to his wife, whom he had married solely for his property, increased every day. She had managed so as to deceive him in her estates, and in this he had been caught in his own snare; she thought herself a Princess, possessed of such an elegant mansion at Venice, and the castle of Gorgono, among the Appenines; to which Androssi talked of going to receive some rents, as he had been absent two years, during which time it had been occupied only by an old steward.

It was not long before the Count Milenza obtained Androssi's permission to pay his addresses to Emily, notwithstanding she gave him most frankly her reasons why they were inadmissible. Androssi was now seldom at home, except when the Count, or Signor Rodoni was there, for between himself and Savilli a coolness seemed to exist, though the latter remained in the house. Rodoni and Androssi were often privately closeted together, and after these intercourses, Emily read in his countenance the deep and dark workings of his mind. A letter about this period found its way from Angereau by the ordinary post to the hands of Emily. It breathed the continuance of his affection, and announced that La Vallée was let to a new tenant; who was to take possession on that day week by Lebas' orders, and that the old Theresa was discharged; since which events he had received a summons to join his regiment. This intelligence was a direct infringement of D'Orville's last injunction, and Emily resolved to remonstrate strongly with M. Lebas on the subject. Androssi soon after mentioned the necessity of her acquiescing in the step her uncle had

[1] Signora Herminia in *Udolpho*, where she is another gifted musician.

taken, seeing it was for her advantage, and it could not be prevented; Emily therefore wrote a few lines at the bottom of a letter Androssi was about to send to him, signifying her assent to be guided by his judgement.

On the following day the Count dined at Androssi's, and appeared unusually gay and confident. In the evening Madame and her party went out upon the sea, and the Count led Emily to his zendaletto,[1] or private barge, carrying her hand to his lips, and thanking her for her condescension. On observing she was quite alone with the Count, she turned to go away, and was met by Androssi, who overruled the delicacy of her objections, and reconducted her to the zendaletto. After the gondoliers had rowed a little way, the Count, taking the hand of Emily, said he did not know how to express his gratitude for her goodness in consenting to his wishes; but his thanks were also due to Signor Androssi, who had allowed him the opportunity of doing so.—Emily regarded her company with a stern look, and demanded of Androssi what was meant by this mystery of consent. Androssi replied, that her affectation of ignorance was inadmissible, when she had that morning written to M. Lebas her assent to a marriage between the Count and herself,—a match highly to her advantage and honour. This induced Emily to give an explanation of the manner in which he had basely appropriated her letter respecting La Vallée to another purpose, and drew from her some remarks on the duplicity of Androssi, and her dislike to the Count. The subject, now placed in a new light, had nearly created an affair of honour[2] between the two friends, but Androssi, moderating his passion, requested the Count would order his servants to row back to Venice, that he might have some private conversation with him. Emily was happy to find herself once more safely returned to her own apartment, and she resolved when M. Lebas came, to interest him, since she could not return to La Vallée, to suffer her to board in a convent in France. In

---

[1] *zendaletto*: while originally denoting a cloth covering for the rear part of a gondola, the term came generally to mean the gondola itself. The OED identifies *The Mysteries of Udolpho* as featuring the first use of the term in this sense, although as Terry Castle has pointed out in her notes on the Oxford University Press edition of *Udolpho*, Radcliffe found the term (where it refers to women's clothing) in one of her travel source books, Hester Lynch Piozzi's popular *Observations and Reflections made in the Course of a Journey through France, Italy, and Germany*, published in 1789 (p. 685, note 197).

[2] affair of honour: a duel.

the meantime she requested Mad. Androssi to use her influence with the Count to discontinue his visits, but she found her aunt warm in his interest.

Androssi now prepared to go to Miarenti, where M. Lebas was, and during the several days which elapsed before the family departed, Emily saw nothing of Count Milenza, which extremely surprised her. Their vessel now proceeded down the Brenta, and Emily sat on the stern by herself, till she was summoned to take refreshment in the cabin, where her aunt was seated, whose angered countenance indicated some recent dispute with her husband. Androssi then spoke to Emily of M. Lebas, and asked whether she meant to disclaim her knowledge of the subject of his letter to him. Emily replied, that she held the truth too sacred to deny it; and then, to avoid further questions, retook her station on the deck. The barge, after being towed a few hours longer, stopped at a flight of marble steps, which led up the bank to a lawn. On landing, they found M. and Mad. Lebas, with a few friends, seated on sofas in the portico, enjoying, according to the custom of the country, the refreshing coolness at two hours past midnight. After the usual introduction, Lebas spoke aside to Androssi on his private affairs, till he named his niece, and then they withdrew to the gardens. The conversation between the two ladies lay upon the superiorities of their own country, which continued till the morning dawned, and exhibited the market boats going to Venice. When the absent gentlemen rejoined the party, they strolled together round the luxuriant gardens, while Emily often lingered behind to contemplate the distant landscape, after which they retired to repose. Emily the next day took the earliest opportunity of speaking with M. Lebas concerning La Vallée: he informed her in a positive tone, that the disposal of the place was a necessary measure to preserve at least a small income for her; and added, that he was happy to hear the Venetian Count had made her such a noble offer, and she had accepted it. Emily now explained the mistake which Androssi had led her into, and her determination to refuse Milenza; this so exasperated the ambitious Lebas, that, he owned, if she persisted in her folly, both himself and Androssi would abandon her to the contempt of the world.

The following night, after a trip on the water, they returned to a splendid supper in the airy hall, when the Count was present. On the following day he renewed his addresses with great warmth, and

Emily, in the most severe manner, gave him a rejection. During her stay at this pleasant villa, Emily was rendered miserable, by the assiduities of Milenza, and the cruelties of Androssi and Lebas, who seemed more determined than ever on effecting the marriage. Lebas at length relinquished his persuasions, and left the business to Androssi, with whom he arranged a plan for the nuptials, proposing to be with him at Venice immediately after they were concluded. The family of Androssi, with the Count, then took their leave, and returned to Venice at midnight, when Androssi and Milenza withdrew to a cassino, and Emily retired to her own apartment. On the following day Androssi, in a short conversation with Emily, informed her, that he would no longer be trifled with, and that the marriage, if necessary, should take place without her consent. He then reminded her that she was a stranger in a foreign country, and that, if she compelled him to become her enemy, the punishment she should receive would exceed her expectation. After he had retired, and Emily had recovered her despair, she resolved to brave his anger, and endure the worst rather than be forced to consent to a hated union. An affair now happened which delayed the marriage for a few days. Androssi's friend, Rodoni, had privately assassinated a nobleman, and the senate having taken up the business, one of the bravos, for the sake of the reward, had confessed his employer's name. Rodoni, therefore, flew to his friend, who secreted him till the energy of justice had relaxed, and he had effected his escape from Venice. On the next evening, Androssi informed Emily that she was to be married the following morning. The evening was far advanced, when Madame Androssi came to her chamber with some bridal ornaments which the Count had sent to Emily, who endeavoured once more to interest her aunt in her favour, but without effect. For some time she sat so lost in thought, as to be wholly unconscious where she was. When her terrors had subsided, she retired to bed, not to sleep, but to collect spirits enough to bear her through the scene of the approaching morning. Emily was awakened from a slumber into which she had sunk, by a quick knocking at her door: it was Alise, who came to tell Emily not to be frightened, but Signor Androssi had sent her to desire she would get ready directly to leave Venice. On demanding the cause of this sudden movement, Alise said that he had just come home in a very ill humour, and called all the servants out of their beds, who reported that his Excellenza was going to his castle in the Appennines. Alise then hastened from the room, and Emily, throwing her clothes and books into a travelling trunk, was ready before Madame Androssi, who appeared to undertake the journey with more reluctance than any one. The family at length embarked, but neither the Count Milenza nor Rodoni was of the party, and Emily felt like a criminal who receives a short respite. When they had landed on the shore, Androssi did not embark on the Brenta, but pursued his way in carriages across the country to the Appennines: during the journey his manner to Emily was uncommonly severe.

When they began to ascend these majestic mountains, the beauty of the wild scenery for a while absorbed the sorrows of our heroine. They continued rising till they entered a narrow pass, which shut out every view of the surrounding country, and placed them in desert and craggy wilds.——Towards the close of the day the road wound into a deep valley, surrounded by shaggy and almost inaccessible steeps. Through an opening of the cliffs the setting sun streamed upon the towers and battlements of a castle, that spread its extensive ramparts on the brow of a precipice above.—"Look!" said Androssi, after a silence of several hours, "there is Gorgono!"—The carriage having passed through a road lined with tall pines, at length emerged upon a heathy rock, and soon reached the gates, where the deep tone of the portal bell gave notice to open the massy gates; after which an ancient servant of the castle drew the bolts, and the carriage passed through one gloomy court yard into another, overgrown with weeds. The mind of Emily was impressed with one of those premature convictions which the reason cannot resist, and which filled her with inward horror. They were led through a large gothic hall to a marble staircase, passing the foot of which they traversed an antichamber, and then entered a spacious apartment, wainscoted with larch-wood. A single lamp illuminated this room, and presented fearfully to the eye the tall figure of Androssi, as he paced the floor, his arms folded, and his countenance shaded by the high plume that waved in his hat. The old servant now entered to welcome his master to the castle, and to inform him, that for want of repair some of the battlements of the north tower had fallen down. A fire being lighted in the hall, the family supped, after which Alise was called to shew Emily to her room: This was called the double chamber, and lay over the south rampart, at the opposite angle to that of Madame. The way to Emily's apartment was up the marble staircase, and through some intricate windings, into which Alise, more intent upon telling her fears than finishing her progress, entered, and became bewildered. Emily now entered a large and spacious apartment, hung with tapestry, which opened to a suite of others, one of which was decorated with pictures. Among these a battle piece attracted her notice: a soldier with a malignant countenance was looking at his fallen foe, who was holding his hand up, supplicating. The countenance struck Emily as resembling Androssi.—Passing on, they came to another, concealed by a veil of black silk: Alise started at the sight of it, and exclaimed, "This, surely, is the picture they told me of at Venice!" Emily bid her remove the veil; but this she positively declined, and walking away with the light, Emily was compelled to follow. All she could learn of Alice[1] was, that something dreadful belonged to it, and that it had been covered up *in black ever since*, and that it somehow had to do with the owner of the castle before Androssi came to the possession of it. At length they regained the marble staircase, and meeting with one of the servants, Emily was conducted to her chamber, which lay at the end of the corridor, near the suite of apartments through which they had been wandering. Caterina having made a fire in the chamber, which was very ancient and large, Alise and she retired to attend on Madame Androssi. Emily now began to examine her chamber, and perceiving a door through which she had not entered, she passed it, and saw a deep narrow staircase; not choosing to descend it at present, she returned to her room, and endeavoured to fasten the door, which had two bolts on the outside, but no security within. This defect she endeavoured to remedy by placing a heavy chair against the door. Emily was soon after cheered by the entry of Alise with some firing and supper, which Madame Androssi had sent her. Emily made the good-natured girl sit down with her, and it was not long before the secret she had acquired from one of the servants, under a promise of secrecy, began to expand itself. "Do you know, Madame," said Alise, "this old castle was not always Signor Androssi's, nor his father's neither; but by some law or other came to the Signor, if the lady died unmarried: This lady used to live in the castle, and the Signor used to come and see her, and offered to

[1] An obvious typographical error for "Alise."

marry her, though he was someway related to her. The lady was in love with somebody else, and would not have him, but pined about the castle for her lover. This happened a good many years ago, when Signor Androssi was a young man. The lady was called Signora Mirandini, and was very handsome.—The Signor finding he could not make her listen to him, left the castle for a long time, and never came near it.—Now it happened one stormy evening, in November, this grand lady walked into the woods, which she loved to do, with her own maid; but, Madame, from that day to this she has never been heard of, and it is reported that she has been seen several times since walking about the castle.—Carolo, the old steward, they say, knows such things, if he would but tell. However, since the lady has disappeared by day, the Signor has taken possession[1] of the castle, and as she has not come to claim it within so many years, it is now his own. The spirit of the lady has been seen several times walking in the unfrequented parts of the castle, but nobody ever saw it come in or go out. They say there is a chapel adjoining the west side of the castle, where such groans are heard at midnight, it makes one shudder to think of them!"—The farther progress of Alise's story was interrupted by the entrance of Catherina,[2] who came to summon her to her mistress. When Alise was gone, Emily endeavoured to console herself to sleep; but her thoughts were so occupied by the strange story she had heard, and the reports Angereau had mentioned, that it was one o' clock before she sunk to sleep. When she awoke, and had surveyed the extent of the castle and the wildness of the surrounding country, from her casement window, her eyes glanced on the door she had so carefully barricadoed[3] the preceding night. Finding the chair had been moved a little way, and that the door was bolted on the other side, she felt as if she had seen an apparition, and determined to request Madame Androssi's leave to change her chamber; but this the latter had not power to do, and, upon her application to Androssi, with a stern malignant countenance he rebuked her for her idle fears.

Alise, the next time she saw Emily, proceeded to ask how Ma'amselle had slept in the double chamber; and stated, that fright-

---

[1] "possien," a typesetter's error, in the original.

[2] A typographical error for "Caterina."

[3] Radcliffe uses "guarded" here.

ful stories were told about that room; and Emily related, that the outside bolts had been fastened during the night. Alise's terror was very visible. Emily; finding her spirits re-assured by the non-arrival of the Count, determined to explore the adjoining chambers of the castle, and, among the rest, the veiled picture. Having proceeded to the room, and paused a moment before she opened the door, she hastily entered, and went towards the picture, the frame of which appeared of an uncommon size. With a timid hand she lifted the veil, but instantly let it fall, perceiving that what it concealed was no picture; and, before leaving the chamber, she dropped senseless on the floor![1] Having recovered herself so far as to get to her own apartment, she placed herself by the casement, and gave way to the horrors that filled her mind, till she was rouzed by the voices of Androssi and his friends speaking chearfully. That day she met them at dinner, but there was a busy seriousness in their looks not usual with them. Androssi evidently laboured under some vexation, during their unsociable meal. When the servants had withdrawn, Emily learned that the Cavalier, whom Rodoni had assassinated, was dead, and strict search was still making for him, which seemed to give Androssi a secret uneasiness.—After dinner, Madam Androssi and Emily retired; the latter went to the ramparts, for her mind had not yet sufficiently recovered from its late shock, to endure the loneliness of her chamber. At night, Alise renewed the conversation about the extraordinary things related of the castle. "Old Carolo," said Alise, "seemed quite astonished, when I told him that the door of the double chamber had been fastened on the outside during the night. He did not tell me why he was so alarmed at your having found it open, but I am sure I would no more sleep in this chamber than on the great cannon at the end of the east ramparts, where a figure several times has been seen to plant itself as if on guard.—That terrible picture, too, which you wanted to see last night, and which my dear Rovedo first told me of,—this morning, do you know, I took a fancy to see it, and got as far as the door, but found it locked."—On enquiry, Emily found it was just after she had entered the chamber, and, from the an-

[1] The veiled picture is one of the most famous icons in early Gothic fiction, as is attested by the very name of this chapbook adaptation, and is the most famous instance of Radcliffe's mastery of suspense and its emotional heightening. As with *Udolpho*, what Emily has just seen behind the veil will not be revealed until much later in the novel.

swers of Alise, it was evident that she and her informer were ignorant of the horrible truth. Emily herself felt also considerably alarmed, lest Androssi should have discovered her visit to the picture.—They sat talking, till the sound of the great bell of the portal alarmed them, and soon after a carriage drove into the court-yard. Emily exclaimed, "It is the Count!" and, on sending Alise to enquire, she returned with the unpleasant intelligence of his arrival; and that, in the way, she had met Rovedo, who said, that Androssi was then counselling with the other Signors, and he was sure something was hatching.—Emily again dispatched Alise to learn what was the object of the Count in visiting the Castle, but she returned, after some time, unsuccessful, not being able to gain intelligence from the servants, who were either ignorant, or affected to be so. Having now dismissed Alise, who complained much of want of sleep, she sat musing till her eye rested on the miniature-picture found after her father's death. It was open upon the table before her, and called up the recollection of the dreadful words in the manuscript. At length, raising herself from her reverie, she lay upon the bed without undressing, and heard the Castle clock strike two, before she closed her eyes. From her disturbed slumber she was soon awakened, by a noise from the door of the staircase; it seemed like that made by the undrawing of rusty bolts, often ceasing, and being renewed. While Emily kept her eyes fixed on the spot, the door slowly opened, and a human figure strongly appeared, as it approached the feeble lamp on the hearth. It then advanced, and having looked between the curtains, it took up the light, and walked to the bed. At this instant, the dog Mignon, which had slept at Emily's feet, awoke; and, barking loudly, flew at the stranger, who struck the animal smartly with a sheathed sword, and, in the moment after, Emily discovered the Count Milenza!—She gazed at him, for a moment, in speechless affright, while he earnestly besought her to fear nothing.—Recovering her faculties, she leaped from the bed in her clothes, ran to the door by which he had entered, and there discovered, by the gleam of a lamp, another man, half way down the steps.—The Count, now taking her hand, led her back to the chamber, and then swore, that what he had done was only dictated by love and despair; that Androssi was a villain, who would have sold her to him; and that, if she meant to avoid his ambition and dreadful machinations, she would not hesitate to fly with one who adored her, and had already taken means for a safe egress from the castle.—Emily remonstrated with him on the impossibility of his ever possessing her affections, and the folly of imagining that she would quit the tyranny of Androssi for that of one who would force her inclinations.—The Count, finding that his arguments were retorted with double force on himself, at last grew outrageous, and swearing by heaven that Androssi should never possess her, he bid her prepare to accompany him to his carriage, whither, if she made any resistance, his servants should force her.—Emily knew, that, in the remote part where she was, no assistance could reach her, and all that remained was to remonstrate. The Count, now advancing to the door of the stair-case, called to Besario, and presently several steps were heard ascending.—Emily uttered a loud shriek—the dog barked—and, at the same moment, the door that opened upon the corridor gave way; and Androssi, followed by the old steward and several others, rushed into the room. "Draw!" cried Androssi to the Count, who did not wait for a second challenge. "This to thine heart, villain!" said the Count, as he made a thrust at his enemy with his sword, who parried the blow; and, after receiving a wound in his own arm, and severely hurting his adversary, disarmed him. The Count then fell back into the arms of his servant, and Androssi held his sword over his fallen antagonist, ready to give the fatal thrust; but Savilli arrested his hand. Androssi then gave orders, that the Count should instantly leave the Castle, and adjourned to examine his own hurt. When the Count recovered, he found Emily bending over him, with an eye of solicitation, and he addressed her—"I have deserved this," said he, "but not from Androssi: from you, Emily, in whom my whole soul centered, I have deserved punishment, and received pity. Forgive the sufferings I have already occasioned you: but, for that villain, Androssi, tell him, that Milenza will not leave another murder on his conscience if he can help it! He shall hear from me again." Having again solicited Emily's pity and pardon, he ordered his servants to convey him to his carriage, and deposit him at the first cottage they came to. Emily sought her aunt, to acquaint her of the affair, but she knew it all; and spoke of her husband's wound with the greatest apathy; after which, Emily, attended by Alise, retired to her chamber, having secured the stair-case door by placing some heavy furniture against it.

It will now be necessary to account for some of the previous transactions. When Milenza went to the house of Androssi, on the morning appointed for his marriage with Emily, he was surprised to find no one there but the old housekeeper; from whom he learned, by threats, that Emily was carried to the Castle of Gorgono, on the Appennine,[1] whither he determined to follow, and obtain either her or full revenge on his enemy,—Milenza had lately received a confirmation that Androssi's circumstances were greatly involved; and, from this cause, he had promoted the Count's suit, the price of which was to be the surrender of the Gascony estate, on the completion of the nuptials. In the mean time, Androssi had learned that Milenza's extravagance had deranged his affairs, and not coming to assign over the deed of cession to Androssi, he concluded that he meant to keep possession, and defraud him. Under this idea, he departed suddenly for Gorgono, and was followed by Milenza, who came to claim Emily, but the Signor, abiding by his first condition, the Count thought to carry her off by stratagem, having learned the path of the private staircase, by bribing a disaffected servant, who had long lived in the castle. Old Carolo, who was on the watch, told his suspicions to his master, and thus the escape of Emily was prevented. The night following the sanguinary transactions in the corridor, Emily passed undisturbed, and, the following morning, Alise told her that old Carolo had just shewn her a picture of the late lady of the place, to [which] she would conduct her. It was in an obscure chamber, and several other portraits hung on the walls, covered with dust and cobwebs. It represented a lady in the flower of youth and beauty; but the countenance wore a haughty impatience of misfortune, and none of that captivating sweetness Emily had looked for. From this room Emily retired to converse with her aunt, whom she found in tears, and whose pride, for the first time, condescended to state her misery, and the present ruined state of her husband's circumstances; as well as his cruel treatment of her.

When Emily retired to her chamber, she had leisure to reflect on the truth of Milenza's words, and hence formed a conviction that Androssi had broken off the match with him that he might dispose of her to a higher purchaser. The next day dinner was served in Emily's apartment by the Signor's orders, and Alise attended, who said the

[1] More commonly spelled "Apennine," referring to the Apennine Mountains in Italy.

same injunction was extended to her lady.

Emily now enquired if she had heard any thing of Count Milenza, and learned that he was lodged in a cottage in the wood below, where he was dangerously ill. Emily expressed some uneasiness for his recovery, and Alise wondered that Emily could feel any concern for one whom she so much disliked: this led to a conversation about Mad. Androssi, and the active part she had taken in persuading her husband to compel the marriage, in the course of which Alise mentioned the many unkind things she had heard her mistress say of Emily's disposition and manners. In the evening Androssi sat late carousing with his guests in the cedar chamber. His recent triumph over Milenza had elevated his spirits, and Valenza, after having drank pretty freely, informed Androssi that the Count had asserted, before he had quitted the castle, that it did not belong to the present possessor, and that he would not willingly leave another murder on his conscience. Androssi asked fiercely if any one believed the assertion of this disappointed knave, and they all replied in the negative. The Signor then said, for their satisfaction, he would briefly relate the way in which he became possessed of Gorgono. "It is now near twenty years," said Androssi, "since this castle became mine. The lady, my predecessor, was distantly related to me by the female line. She was beautiful and rich; I wooed her, but her heart was fixed upon another, and she rejected me. It is probable, however, she was disliked by the person she approved of, for she afterwards fell into a deep melancholy, and there is reason to think she put a period to her own life. I was not at the castle at the time. As some mysterious circumstances attended that event, I will repeat them." "Repeat them!" said a voice. The guests looked astonished, and Androssi exclaimed—"We are overheard!"—They searched the chamber, and finding no person but themselves, Valenza desired him to proceed. In a lower tone he then continued—"Signora Mirandini had for some months shewn a disturbed mind. In one of the gloomy nights of November she retired to the double chamber, and from that hour was seen no more!" "Seen no more! her body never found!" exclaimed Brandolo and the rest. "Never!" replied Androssi. "And you suspected her of suicide?" said Valenza, looking keenly at the Signor;—"on what ground pray?"—"I will tell you hereafter," continued Androssi.—"I now come to a very extraordinary circumstance, which demands your attention and secrecy." "Attend!" cried the voice, and the company started from their chairs. Every one heard the exclamation, and rushed out of the room, but nothing appeared that could create any alarm. Androssi proposed to drop the subject, and bidding them retire to their apartments, he left them, as he said, to dive into the mystery.

We now return to Angereau, whom we left at Thoulouse.—Having, after several visits to La Vallée, joined his battalion, he went to Paris.—His pure manners and unadulterated notions soon raised a little conspiracy against him on the part of his brother officers, to reduce his morality to their gay level. He began to visit the fashionable circles of Paris, and among the rest made one at the *petit soupers*[1] of the Countess Monge,[2] whose beauty, taste, and talents, were unrivalled. There was also a Marchioness Decamp,[3] at whose assemblies he passed much of his time.—Her parties were less elegant and more vicious than those of the Countess Monge. These vortexes of elegance and dissipation had much weakened the force Emily had on his affections, and he endeavoured as much as he could to prevent her intruding on his thoughts, because he was sensible he had departed from the purity of conduct which could alone make him worthy of her. In this state we shall leave Angereau, and turn to the gloomy Appenines, where the thoughts of Emily were still faithful to her lover.

Androssi had endeavoured to trace the late mysterious voice, but could resolve it into nothing else than a trick of the servants.—In the mean time Madame Androssi remained closely confined in her room, visited only by Emily and Alise. The latter, coming one day to Emily's apartment, asked her with concern, if she knew the meaning of having so many strange ill-looking people quartered about the castle, and why the fortifications were put into such repair, when there seemed no foe to contend with, and why the Signor held so many midnight counsels, and received these cut-throat looking men, if it were not to do more murders in the Castle?

Alise having finished her tale, left the chamber, to find out new wonders. Emily that night, as she was retiring to rest, was alarmed by a strange and loud knocking at her chamber door, against which a heavy weight fell, as if it would burst it open. She called to know

---

[1] "Little" or small, informal dinners.

[2] Countess Lacleur in *Udolpho*, where she is described as "a woman of eminent beauty and captivating manners" (Volume II, Chapter 8).

[3] The Marchioness Champfort in *Udolpho*.

who was there, but no voice answered. As thus she stood, fearful lest some assassin might enter, at the staircase door, she heard a faint breathing near her. She was proceeding to her casement to call for assistance, when a footstep seemed to be upon the staircase, and she rushed to the door she had quitted; hastily opening it, she fell over the body of Alise, who had fallen into a fit, and was conveyed by Emily into her chamber. When she had recovered, Alise affirmed, that she had seen a tall figure gliding along into the room that was always shut up, and of which nobody kept the key but the Signor.—"Was it the chamber where the black veil hangs?" asked Emily. "No," replied Alise, "it was one nearer to this room," and Emily now recollected the footsteps she had just heard on the stone staircase. Alise slept that night with Emily, and nothing further was heard. On the following morning, from an upper casement Emily saw a complete band of armed men on horseback, headed by Brandolo and Valenza, depart from the castle, and she remarked that the fortifications seemed to be complete, the workmen being no longer employed. The mystery was soon developed by the arrival of the talkative Alise, who had learned, as a great secret from Rovedo, her lover, that the Signor was going to be the Captain of this gang of banditti. Alise continued so long relating her fears and Rovedo's stories, that Madame Androssi sent for Emily, to be a witness that she refused to give up the estates which had been conferred to her previous to her last marriage. Androssi insisted on having the writings made over to him, and his wife as resolutely persisted in refusing. Androssi looked at her for a moment with a stern and steady countenance. "You shall be removed this night to the eastern turret;" said he: "there you will learn the danger of offending the Lord of Gorgono."

Androssi then left them, and Emily not long after interceded with him for her aunt, and obtained this condition, that, if she would sign the writing, she should escape imprisonment in the eastern turret, where, if she once entered, a dreadful punishment would await her. This Emily reported to her aunt, and, waving all consideration of the loss that would arise to herself as her aunt's heir, she persuaded her to give up the estates. Madame Androssi wished, she said, to have retained them for the benefit of her niece and Angereau, and paid a high compliment to the generous sentiments of Emily.—When she quitted Madame at night to retire to rest, her way lay by the chamber where Alise had been terrified. Her alarm made her hesitate at the door of the chamber, whence issued the sound of a human voice; in a moment after which Androssi came out, and directly retreated, but not before Emily had seen a person sitting by the fire in a melancholy attitude. While she watched, the door was again opened, and as quickly closed. Emily then retreated to her own chamber, and received that night no other interruption, except from the people in the castle exchanging the watch word as in a regular garrison. The next morning Emily waited on Madame Androssi, who had formed the resolution of escaping with her niece, in preference to giving up her estates, on which she might then enjoy life comfortably. Androssi entered the room while they were in conversation, and demanded if she had resolved upon his proposal; upon her hesitating he gave her till the evening to decide, and added that as he expected a party of cavaliers to dinner, he should expect her to sit at the head of the table with Emily, fully dressed for the occasion. The blush that overspread Emily's countenance when she entered the dinner hall, where the guests were sitting, added to her beauty, and made her look irresistible. Two of the cavaliers then rose, and seated her between them. The eldest was a tall man, with a long and narrow visage, and eyes dark and penetrating. He was about forty, and had a subtle look and harsh features. The rest of the guests, in number eight, were dressed in uniforms, and all had the fierce looks of banditti. During the dinner they talked of war and the Doge of Venice.[1] When this repast was over, they rose, and each filling his goblet with wine, drank "Success to our exploits!" Androssi was lifting his goblet to drink, when suddenly the wine hissed, rose to the brim, and burst the glass into a thousand pieces. He always used that sort of Venice glass which had the quality of breaking upon receiving poisoned liquor;[2] instantly therefore he exclaimed, "Shut the gates!—There is a traitor among us; let the innocent assist in discovering the guilty!" The cavaliers all drew their swords, and Madame Androssi quitted the hall. The servants, being summoned, uniformly declared their ignorance of the design; it therefore appeared, as the goblet of Androssi alone was poisoned, that the two servants who distributed the wine must be

---

[1] The Doge was the ruling official of Venice, which at the time in which the story is set was one of the powerful and independent "city-states" of Italy.

[2] A medieval superstition about Venetian crystal drinking vessels held that they were so pure they would shatter if exposed to poison.

privy to it: these therefore he ordered to be chained in a dungeon till they confessed; after which, in about half an hour, he followed his wife to her dressing-room.—"It avails you nothing," said he to her, "to deny the fact.—Your only chance of mercy rests on a full confession; for your accomplice has confessed the deed." Emily piteously interceded with the Signor, while Madame Androssi insisted it was only a subterfuge on her husband's part to take her life. Some person now calling to him, with a dreadful menace he left the room, and locked them both in it, leaving them to comfort each other.

They were a short time after alarmed by the voice of Alise, requesting immediate entrance, as the Signors and Androssi were all fighting below in the hall, and were now coming towards her. As Emily could not open the door, she bid the poor girl fly, and in an instant they heard no more of her. Madame had just time to exclaim "Heaven protect us, I hear them coming!" when Androssi unlocked the door, and rushed in, followed by the three ruffian-looking men, whom he ordered directly to seize and carry her away. Emily sunk senseless on a couch, and when she recovered, no one was with her. Wishing now to gain information of the fate of her aunt, she stepped into the gallery, and proceeded to the smaller hall; everywhere as she passed, she heard from a distance the uproar of contention. Perceiving it was useless to seek her aunt through the intricacies of the castle, she was about to leave this dismal hall, when she drew aside, on seeing a wounded man borne slowly along by four others. His groans vibrated on her ear till they were lost in the distance, as she explored the way to her chamber. Her mind was employed in various conjectures on the fate of Madame Androssi till sun-set, when she determined to penetrate if possible to the eastern turret, a resolution which was for a while checked by the dread of some ruffian meeting her on the stone staircase, or encountering the mysterious inhabitant of the neighbouring apartment. About twelve o'clock, having lighted her lamp from some embers on the hearth, and secured the staircase door, she crossed into a passage that went along the south side of the building to the staircase, as she thought, leading to the turret. At the end of the gallery she came to two flights of steps, one of which she chose from chance; it opened into a wide passage, in a chamber of which she heard the voice of Alise calling out for Rovedo, who, it appeared, had locked her up there for safety, and, having been since wounded in the affray of the previous night, had not been able to liberate her. Emily promised to interest old Carolo for her, and then obtained a direction from her to the eastern turret.—Having reached the stairs at the bottom of it, she began to ascend, and perceived the steps were stained with blood to the summit, where a fastened door prevented her from any farther entrance. Emily had little doubt her aunt was here, and she called on her name without receiving any answer. Finding further pursuit impracticable at present, she descended the turret, and regained her own apartment, when wearied nature sunk to repose.

It was near noon next day before Emily ventured from her room, and the first visit she paid was to Alise, who earnestly intreated to be saved from starving and the horrors of loneliness. In returning to the great hall, she met the Signor, and intreated him to inform her where her aunt was placed, and to send Carolo to liberate Alise. To the latter he readily consented, but bid her not interfere in the fate of the former, who was taken care of.—A trumpet now sounding, Androssi went forth to see the occasion of it, and sent old Carolo to Emily, who informed her that Valenza and his party had just arrived, and that the fight between the Signor and his guests, about the suspicion of poison he had thrown out, was now amicably settled. He then liberated Alise, whose only concern was for the wounds Rovedo had received in the affray. Two days more passed without any material occurrence: on the last night she was looking out of her casement at a late hour, and contemplating the wildness of the views surrounding her, when she observed the star rise which had always accompanied the magical music she had heard in Languedoc. Suddenly the same sounds were repeated, and she endeavoured to ascertain from what quarter they proceeded, but whether from a room of the castle or from the terrace, she could not with certainty judge.—Having staid till the harmony had ceased, she closed the casement, and went to bed. Alise came almost breathless to Emily's apartment the following morning, to announce that the person whom she had seen sitting in the chamber from which Androssi had emerged at midnight, was no other than Signor Rodoni, who had flown from Venice for the assassination of the nobleman. Emily now asked if any news had been heard of her aunt, but Alise knew nothing, and supposed she was disposed of in the same manner as the first lady of the Castle.—There was another important mission Alise had to communicate in great confidence, which was, that the porter of the Castle, Barbaro, earnestly desired to speak with her, and would attend for that purpose on the eastern rampart at midnight. Emily bid her tell him that she would meet him there herself at the appointed hour.—Emily's thoughts till the hour of interview were much occupied in conjecturing whether the conversation of Barbaro related to her aunt or herself.—At midnight they reached the first terrace, and having passed the centinels, they proceeded to the eastern rampant, where Barbaro arrived a few minutes after them. He made Alise retire, and then, having enjoined Emily to secresy, said, "Lady, if it were known I had betrayed my trust, my life would answer for it.—I have heard from Alise your anxiety to hear of Madame Androssi, and I have to inform you that she is now my prisoner, shut up in the chamber over the great gates of the court, where I will conduct you to a sight of the prisoner, if you will repair to the postern gate of the Castle, the following night at two, when the Signor is at rest.—Emily commended her aunt to his pity, and promised to reward him handsomely for the indulgence. The murdering countenance of this man almost gave a falsity to the possibility of his doing a generous act; nevertheless much was to be gained by the hazard, if he were sincere; but if not, might it not be a snare to destroy her in the same manner as her aunt? Dismissing however the belief of such enormous turpitude, she resolved to go at the fixed time.—At one o'clock that night she opened her casement, but, though she saw the star rise, no music floated in the air;[1] all was hushed till the Castle clock tolled two, and Emily stole from her apartment to meet Barbaro at the postern gate. After chiding her for delay, Barbaro unclosed the gate, and they passed into a long passage, by torch light; at the end he unlocked a door, when they descended a few steps into a chapel, which appeared to be in ruins, and of which Alise had before told her with much terror. Emily's heart sunk as she followed him: he turned out of the principal aisle of the church to some steps that led to the vaults. Here she saw an open grave, which Emily concluded was prepared for her aunt. They however ascended another flight of stairs, passed through some gloomy chambers, and at length arrived at the postern door, and ascended a pair of winding stairs.—This conducted to a chamber, in which Barbaro said he

[1] This is the end of Volume II of *Udolpho*.

should leave Emily for a few minutes.—Taking the lamp, she began to reconnoitre the dark and mouldering room; in the centre was an iron chair with a chain suspended over it, probably the suffering place of some unfortunate. Advancing further, she saw a curtain, which extended across the breadth of the room. Thinking it concealed some door, she drew it aside, and discovered a corpse stretched on a kind of couch. She gazed at the ghostly face for a second or two, and then sunk senseless on the floor. In this state Barbaro found her when he returned, and, taking her in his arms, he carried her without the castle walls; the fresh air now revived her, and she beheld herself surrounded by some horsemen, who were just about to lift her on a horse, when Androssi and his men rushed through the portal gate, attacked the cavaliers, defeated the strange horsemen, and returned with Emily to the Castle.—She was immediately sent to her apartment, with Alise to attend her. The late dreadful discovery of the corpse had much injured her intellects, and she required the most soothing treatment to restore her deranged faculties.—Barbaro had been Milenza's instrument in seizing Emily. He had learned from Alise that Emily's anxiety to see her aunt would easily draw her to the postern gate, where the Count had a party of armed men ready to escort her away. The scheme however had failed, from the vigilance of those on watch in the Castle; and Milenza, now recovered from his wounds, and still enamoured of Emily, set off for Venice, projecting new schemes of punishing Androssi, and liberating the injured sufferer.

The following day, Emily was much better, and having dismissed Alise for the night, she stood at the casement, inhaling the cool air till the hour in which the aerial music appeared. While she listened, a low sound saluted her ear, like the soft moans of a person in distress, and presently after a tall figure advanced along the rampart, and placed itself opposite her window, and there remained stationary. Terrified at the gliding form, she was about to retreat from the window, when it started away, and was lost in the obscurity of night. This extraordinary circumstance occupied Emily's attention a great part of the night, and ere she sunk to rest, she resolved to be at the casement on the following one. She saw nothing the next morning of Androssi, who was gone on an excursion with his corps of banditti, and with anxious hope and fear she waited till the time of midnight arrived, but saw nothing on this night. The next day she had an interview with Androssi, and requested him to permit her to retire to France; at the same time boldly challenging him with the murder of his wife. Androssi peremptorily refused the first, and confessed that if she wished to see the latter, as she had so much affection for her, she was to be found lying in the eastern turret.

It was not long before the captains of the banditti began to disagree.[1] The bold manly spirit of Valenza could but ill brook the cruelty and cowardice of Rodoni; which generated a quarrel between the two, and was appeased only outwardly by their comrades. Emily, having learned where her aunt lay, ascended with Alise to the door of the eastern turret, which she had before found fastened; it was now opened, and admitted her into a dusky silent chamber, in which was a bed. A voice saluted her, which she knew to be Madame Androssi's, whose pale and emaciated figure she now recognised. The blood she had seen on the stairs was that of one of the wounded men who had carried her there; and the dead body in the portal chamber was a soldier who had fallen in the affray. Androsssi had removed his wife to the turret, the more quietly to dispatch her, if any circumstance rose to prove her guilt, though he now attributed the poison to some artifice of the Count Milenza. Want of sustenance, and the sorrows of Madame Androssi's mind, had brought her to the verge of death; and all that Emily could effect with the Signor was, to let her be removed and die in her own chamber.—This being effected, Emily would have sat up with her aunt, but the latter insisted on her retiring to her own bed for a few hours, and if any alteration took place for the worse, Alise should apprise her of it. A little after twelve Emily withdrew, and again placed herself at the casement, when the same figure presented itself on the rampart before her, and beckoned to her. While she looked with awe and astonishment, it beckoned again, and Emily asked, "Who is it that wanders at this late hour?" The figure then raised its head, and darted down the terrace, where

---

[1] This is one of the clumsier editorial moments in the chapbook as the redactor tries to bypass a scene in which Montoni and his cohorts have a violent argument that comes to blows and narrowly avoids bloodshed (Volume III, Chapter 3 in *Udolpho*). The redactor has provided no build-up to this moment, having edited out any mention of the fact Montoni/Androssi was meeting with his companions when Emily came to speak with him, and provides so little follow-up in the next sentence that this moment is thoroughly out-of-place.

it disappeared. While she stood musing, the two sentinels walked up the rampart in earnest conversation; the subject of which was, that one of their comrades had fallen down senseless with terror at the sight of a spectre which had alarmed them on a previous night.

In the morning Emily found her aunt just expiring, but still with powers sufficient to place in her hands the papers which would secure to her the estates in France; these Androssi had not yet forced her to sign, and which had been the principal source of her inhuman treatment. At midnight Emily again stole away to her casement, and presently saw a blazing light moving backward and forward at a little distance. As it approached closer, she heard a footstep, and calling out to know who it was, was answered that it was Bolorio, a soldier on guard. "What light is that, which accompanies you," said Emily. "I cannot tell," said the man. "It has hovered over the point of my lance just as you see it all this night. But what it portends heaven only knows."[1] Emily, after a little farther conversation, dismissed the centinel, and was soon after alarmed by the entry of Alise, who came to announce that Madame Androssi was dying. Before they could return to her chamber, she had expired, and all that remained to her excellent niece was to attend the body of this ambitious unfortunate woman, which was deposited on the second night in the grave Emily had seen in the vaults under the chapel. The ceremony was performed by a priest, who, when the service was over, wished to speak with Emily, but was prevented by the presence of their barbarian attendants. This pious Monk belonged to a convent at a little distance, whither Androssi had sent for him to perform the last holy rites. The sight of this good man renewed in Emily the most anxious desire to escape from the castle, but this idea was soon absorbed in others of greater importance. The day after the burial Androssi sent for Emily,

---

[1] This is an allusion (more developed in *Udolpho*), to St. Elmo's fire, a meteorological phenomenon most commonly associated with sailing ships. But the Roman Emperor Julius Caesar's (100 - 44 B.C.E.) *Commentaries on the Gallic and Civil Wars* (in a section not authored by Caesar himself) reports that one night after a violent hailstorm "the shafts of the javelins belonging to the fifth legion, of their own accord, took fire" (*The African Wars*, section 47). Produced by atmospheric electricity during or just before storms, and typically appearing on pointed objects such as the tips of masts or soldier's pikes, St. Elmo's fire usually appears in the "tapering" form to which Emily refers in *Udolpho*, not in a "blazing" form, which surely is an exaggeration. In *Udolpho* the flame is interpreted by Montoni's guards as a bad omen, although traditionally St. Elmo's fire is regarded as a good omen in most circumstances.

and in the presence of Rodoni, requested her, after a few arguments on the natural descent of his wife's property to him, to sign a paper to that effect; but Emily, who immediately discerned the use he meant to make of her signature, decidedly refused, and she was bid to retire. While she sat musing, a peal of laughter rose from the terrace, and on going to the casement, she perceived three Italian ladies, one of whom was Signora Tessini, whose agreeable manners she had so much esteemed at Venice.—Quite at a loss to guess what motive could have brought them to the Castle, she formed an idea that they were come to be mistresses to some of the cavaliers, and the subsequent entertainment that Androssi gave that night, with the remarks Alise made on their behaviour, confirmed her in that opinion.

While Androssi and his mistress, for such Signora Tessini now appeared to be, were lost in merriment and revelry, Emily kept close within her chamber, and at the usual hour attended at her casement, when the figure again appeared, and played an air on the lute, accompanying it with the words of a French song, both which she recollected to be the same with those which had formerly so charmed her in the fishing-house at La Vallée. A thought now darted into her mind like lightning, that it was Angereau. She called from the casement to know, if the song was from Gascony, but no answer was returned; and after repeating the question, and finding the unknown performer had ceased to play, she retired to rest, filled with a thousand conjectures on the possibility of its being Angereau, who was perhaps made a prisoner in the endeavour to rescue her. Androssi again repeated his threats to use force if Emily refused to sign the papers; during their conversation they were interrupted twice by a mysterious voice, which the Signor affected not to notice, but left her abruptly to visit the ramparts, and prepare for the approaching siege, which Emily had learned the castle was to undergo. The neighbouring noblemen had taken arms, in consequence of their villas being plundered, and having traced the marauders, were marching towards the castle. This account was in a few hours after confirmed by the presence of old Carolo, who came by the Signor's orders to bid Emily prepare to leave the castle that day, under an escort of his men.—The order was so quick, that she had scarcely time to contemplate the destiny she was next to be moved into, before she found herself outside the walls, and felt no other regret at quitting that gloomy abode than what arose from the fear that the musical figure she had heard was Angereau, and that she was leaving him a prisoner in the castle.

During several hours they travelled on through regions of profound solitude, and winding down precipices, intermixed with forests of cypress, pine, and cedar, till they lost sight of Gorgono. The men, under whose charge Emily was placed, had by their conversation been assassins, and she much feared their object was to dispatch her. As night advanced, they encountered a tremendous storm of thunder and lightning, just as they had nearly descended the mountains. Having arrived in the plains, they proceeded through a chesnut wood to a cottage, the owner of which, on knocking at the door, immediately descended, and let them in. From the manner in which he received Emily's conductors, it was evident that he was apprised of her coming. His wife, whose name was Pattesa, then led her to a neat chamber, where fatigue brought on the sweets of repose. The next morning she found that Borgo, one of her conductors, remained at the cottage, and on her proposing to walk about its vicinity, he forbad it. The owner of this cottage possessed it by the gift of Androssi, for an essential service he had rendered him about eighteen years before, and when Emily had learned this intelligence from their daughter Mariana, she thought herself placed in the hands of one of the murderers of Signora Mirandini, as the periods of the service and that lady's disappearance agreed so well together. The innocent conversation of Mariana often amused the melancholy hours of Emily, and when Borgo so far relaxed as to permit her to walk out in his protection, she always accompanied her; then Emily began to relish the beauties of the country, and the sea, to which the cottage lay very near, afforded by its prospect some compensation for the limited liberty she enjoyed.

The Count Milenza, during these transactions, had been seized at Venice, and placed in a dungeon, in consequence of an anonymous letter sent by Androssi, charging him with treasonable practices. The armed force which had assailed the castle of Gorgono being, after an obstinate resistance, defeated, joy again filled the breast of Androssi, and he sent an escort for Emily, who was removed from the Tuscan cottage, and re-conducted to the Castle. She wished to avoid the presence of Androssi, who with his party were deeply carousing. While she waited to see Alise at the top of the stairs, two of the chiefs rushed out, and demanding of Androssi the way to Emily's room, and commenced a race towards it. Valenza, however, distanced his competitor, while Emily, gliding softly to an angle, met Alise, who conducted her to her own chamber, which lay at another quarter of the Castle. Here Rovedo was introduced to her, the brave gallant of Alise; he promised to defend Emily from the passions of the Signor Valenza, and to effect her escape when it could be done with a probability of safety.

The following morning Androssi summoned Emily to his room, to know if she would sign the papers; she stipulated that she would, if permission were given her, to set off [for] France, as the condition of her consent. This he solemnly swore to do, and she accordingly put her name to the instrument of cession: but, when she claimed the fulfilment of the conditions, he replied that he should not execute that part of the treaty, till he was in full possession, and then ordered Emily to her chamber. The following night Alise and Emily heard the music and the French song repeated, but it seemed to come from so remote a quarter of the castle, that their loudest call could obtain nothing more than a faint articulation in reply. Re-assured, however, by this circumstance, Alise bid Rovedo enquire what prisoners were in the castle, and he brought word that a Frenchman was among them, whom he had conversed with, and whose joy seemed at the most extravagant height when he mentioned Emily's name. "He then gave me this case," said Rovedo, "and told me to tell you, that he would not part with it for worlds, unless it were in the hope of receiving it from your hand again."

Emily took the case, and found it contained the very picture of herself, which her mother had lost in the fishing-house. Her joy was extreme: no doubt existed it was Angereau, and she bid Rovedo tell him as soon as possible she would see him in the corridor, the management of which she left to that faithful domestic, whose only opportunity depended on certain centinels being on guard. On the second night the interview was effected by Rovedo; he introduced the stranger to the apartment, and Emily fainted as she approached to rush into his arms. When she recovered, the French gentleman still held her in his grasp, but it was not Angereau! "Madam," said he, "it is evident you have mistaken me for one more happy.—My name is La Fleur; I am a native of Gascony, and have long admired and loved you. My family residing near La Vallée, I loved to wander near the haunts you frequented; I need not, therefore, disguise, that I visited the fishing-house, and thus became possessed of the picture which I committed to your messenger." Emily now explained the mistake under which she had laid from his not sending his name. The generous La Fleur then made her an offer of his service to assist her in escaping, and thus possess her gratitude, if he could not her love.

While they were conversing, Rovedo entered the room in a great hurry, and bid them follow him instantly, as the outer gates were then open for the sortie of the troops, and, by favour of the darkness, they might escape unobserved. Taking Alise in their way, they reached the portal without being discovered, and detaching two accoutred[1] horses, which stood waiting for their riders, they passed through the dreadful barrier, and took the road that led to the woods, placing the females on the horses, which Rovedo and La Fleur conducted. In this manner they continued that night and the next day, till they descended into the beautiful vale of Arno, whence they proceeded to Florence. As they journeyed, Emily was told by La Fleur that he had been captured in an engagement with Androssi, and had learned from a centinel, whom he had bribed, that the woman he so dearly esteemed was a prisoner like himself.—"This man," continued La Fleur, "permitted me to walk sometimes on the terrace, and I, observing that a light came from a window just over my dungeon, I concluded it was you: for the purpose of exciting your attention, I procured an old lute, and accompanied it with my voice; but from the distance I was at I twice only thought I received an answer. The dungeon in which I lay was parted by a thin partition from a room where Androssi held his nocturnal counsels, and more than once I have endeavoured to alarm his conscience by repeating his words in a hollow voice, for I am convinced, from his conversation, that he is a murderer."

In this manner he related all the little events which had taken place at the castle, till they arrived at Leghorn, where they took shipping for Marseilles, near which place lay also the regiment of La Fleur, whose reserved conduct excited Emily's esteem, though she could not love him.—Crossing the Gulf of Lyons, they were overtaken by a storm, and wrecked on a part of the Mediterranean coast,

[1] Fully equipped for riding.

near to the castle of Le Blanc, formerly occupied by the Marquis de Lormel, and at which D'Orville had endeavoured to obtain relief in his tour round the sea coast. Since that period it had been occupied by the Count Amant, his relative and heir. The distress of our travellers was immediately relieved by the count, who invited them to the chateau, and found in La Fleur an old acquaintance. Lady Blanche, the Count's daughter, endeared herself to Emily, while Lady Amant took care of Rovedo and Alise. Emily wrote the following day to Angereau; and, in wandering over the grounds with Blanche, perceived it was the same castle which had excited her curiosity so much from the description of Lavoie. Shocked at this discovery, Emily asked Blanche if the nocturnal music was still heard in the environs of the chateau. Blanche, who had never heard of it, enquired of Alithea, the old housekeeper, who said that it was heard at intervals, and had been so ever since her dear lady died eighteen years ago, which was the reason of the late Marquis deserting the castle. "The suite of rooms beyond the gallery contain strange things, my lady," said Alithea. "How like is this young lady to my late mistress, and when she smiles it is her very face! She soon lost her gaiety when she came here. I saw her on her death bed, and never shall forget what she said." Emily thought there was a mystery about this suite of rooms which must be explored. Just then she remembered the veiled picture she had witnessed in the castle of Gorgono, and, by an odd coincidence, the dreadful words that had accidentally met her eye in the MS. papers, and she shuddered at the reference they seemed to bear to the castle of Le Blanc. Being summoned to wait on the Count, he in a paternal manner requested Emily to postpone her idea of entering the convent of St. Clair, and remain with his daughter for a few days. In the mean time Emily wrote to her uncle Lebas, and to the Abbess of the convent, and visited the good old Lavoie. In a few days after, she withdrew to the monastery, and there received a letter from Lebas, stating that the term for which La Vallée had been let was nearly expired; that the affairs of M. Moreau were likely to be arranged to her advantage, and, after giving her an order on a merchant at Narbonne for some money, he advised her to remain at the convent. In a few days Emily, at the request of Lady Blanche, returned with her to the chateau, when the friendship of the Count induced Emily to lay open her affairs to him in a candid and explicit manner.

On the following morning Emily had laid some papers on the table, and with them the miniature picture found in her father's purse. Alithea chanced to enter, and surveying the portrait, exclaimed, "It is the very likeness of my deceased mistress!"—Emily directly concluded the papers destroyed had related to the Marchioness, and as Alithea seemed to know all the particulars, she assured her of secrecy, if she would impart the substance of what she knew. Alithea promised to visit Emily that night, when the family had retired to rest. Till that time, she accompanied Blanche to see a merry-making of the vintagers hard by.—The Count and his lady were highly entertained, and joined the festive dance: but Emily stole away to wander in the adjoining avenue, overcome by the recollection, that, on that day twelvemonth, she had, with her father, beheld the same mirth and been on the same spot. As she walked up a row of chesnuts, she thought she heard the voice of Angereau with Henri, the son of the Count. She turned round—it was indeed Angereau, and she fainted senseless in his arms![1]—Angereau had received Emily's letter, lost no time in repairing to Le Blanc, where he was immediately introduced to the family of the Count on their leaving the vintagers. Having returned to the chateau, Emily remarked, with some surprise, that the Count did not invite Angereau to sleep there, and he went away to his solitary inn, after having heard from Emily the sufferings she had undergone in the castle of Gorgono. When he had retired, the Count explained to Emily the motive of his cool reception of Angereau, having learned from his son, Henri, when at Paris, many anecdotes of his former conduct, marked by a strong tendency to gaming and libertinism.[2]

This intelligence extremely distressed Emily, and when she saw Angereau the following morning, he read in her looks the displeasure she felt at his conduct, which he had no doubt the Count had detailed. He entered into an impassioned avowal of the constancy of his love, and acknowledged the errors he had committed, and the ruin

[1] Radcliffe, as befits her character and personal sense of propriety, showed much more restraint in this scene: when Emily discovers that the voice she has heard indeed belongs to Valancourt, Radcliffe writes "It was, indeed, he! and the meeting was such as may be imagined, between persons so affectionate, and so long separated as they had been." It is the case, however, that Emily faints when she is told that Valancourt was twice imprisoned in Paris—a detail not in the chapbook.

[2] This marks the end of Volume III of *Udolpho*.

he was in, with such an ingenuousness and promise of amendment, that the arguments of Emily gave way to the pleasure of forgiveness, and before the interview was closed, she promised not wholly to discard him.

That night Alithea did not come according to her promise, and Emily was too absorbed with the idea of Angereau to investigate any other subject. The following morning the Count renewed his arguments with Emily to persuade her from farther intimacy with Angereau, till he had passed some time of probation and repentance,—and she might be able to judge by his reformed conduct, if he sincerely loved her. Emily approved the hard lesson, and when Angereau came on the following afternoon, and she announced her resolution of not seeing him again, he applauded the justice of her decision, acknowledged that till he had retrieved his character and fortune he was unworthy to possess her, and then, with a look of despair, he pressed her hand and hurried out of the room, leaving Emily in a state of mental agitation too great to be described. We now return to Androssi, whose band of armed men were attacked by a chosen body of troops in an ambuscade.—This corps had been sent by the State of Venice, at the instigation of Milenza, who obtained his liberty in consequence of Androssi and Rodoni, the assassin, being defeated and made captives.—This business was managed so suddenly that it never reached the ears of Emily; who found the benevolence of a father and a sister in the kindnesses of the Count and his daughter Blanche. Alithea now reminded Emily of the story she was to relate, and the latter appointed that night for the disclosure. Soon after twelve, Alithea entered, and drawing her chair close to Emily, thus began:—

"It is about twenty years since my lady Marchioness came a bride to the chateau, and then she was very like you.—I soon perceived though she smiled she was not happy at heart. My Lord the Marquis kept open house for a long time, but my lady was not happy.—Her father, it seems, had married her to the Marquis for his money, while there was another nobleman, or chevalier, whom she liked better. Among the many visitors who came to our Castle, there was one whose grace and civility seemed just suited to my Lady; and I always remarked that the Marquis seemed very gloomy, and my Lady much depressed when he came. I have heard it said that the Marchioness was privately married to some gentleman before she had the Marquis, and was afraid to own it to her father, who was a very stern man—but I never gave faith to this story. The Marquis at length ill-treated my lady exceedingly, and at the end of a year she was taken ill, and I fear did not come fairly by her death."

While Alithea spoke, the music which had excited Emily's attention at the time of her father's decease, softly stole upon her ear, and Alithea remarked it was the same she had so often heard. She then continued:—"It was one night shortly after my lady's death, when I had been sitting up late, that I first heard this music, which was accompanied by a voice, and exactly resembled the sweet performance of my lady when alive. Sometimes I have not heard it for many months, but still it has returned. When my lady was taken very ill, and shrieked so piercingly, the doctor was sent for, but he arrived too late. He appeared greatly shocked to see her, for soon after her death a frightful blackness overspread her features, and the Marquis was closeted with him for several hours. The body was buried in the convent yonder, and my Lord became melancholy. Soon after he joined his regiment, and never returned again to the chateau, which has been shut up from that time till the present Count became possessed of it by the Marquis's death, which happened in the north of France." Alithea now mentioned another portrait of the Marchioness, hanging up in the suite of rooms where she had died, and which had been shut up for many years. Emily felt a strong desire to view the whole; and on the following night, Alithea attended with the keys of the apartments, which extended along the north side of the chateau. At one o'clock in the morning, taking a lamp, they crossed the servants' hall, and ascended the back staircase, a door upon which was unlocked, and led through several rooms to one more spacious than the rest, crossing which, Alithea unlocked the chamber in which the late Marchioness had died. Every thing remained in its unaltered state, and the pall of black velvet covered the bed in which she expired. In a closet of the chamber was the portrait of the Marchioness, the melancholy of which resembled the miniature: about the shelves lay her various articles of apparel, and on the table was her lute, a crucifix, and a prayer-book open. Having returned into the chamber, she desired once more to look upon the bed: when they came opposite to the open door leading to the saloon, Emily thought she saw something glide in the obscure part of the room.—Overcome by what she conceived only a weakness, she sat down on the side of the bed to recover herself.—Alithea was pointing out the spot where her mistress lay, when to the eyes of Emily the pall appeared to rise and fall.—Alithea saw the motion, and affirmed it was only the wind.—Scarcely, however, had she uttered these words, when it became more strongly agitated than before. Emily, ashamed of being terrified at what might be the mere action of the wind, stepped back, and she gazed within the curtains, the pall moved again, and the apparition of a human countenance rose above it. Screaming with terror they both fled, and alarmed the servants in their way. Having reached their own apartments, they remained together all night, and on the following morning locked up the northern apartments.

Among the visitors at the chateau were the Baron de St. Foix, an old friend of the Count, and the Chevalier his son, who had seen the Lady Blanche at Paris, and had fallen in love with her. The young man had now come with his father to pay his addresses, which were not ill received.—One evening as Emily sat in one of the most sequestered parts of the chateau wood till a late hour, the music and voice she had before heard at midnight stole upon her ear; they approached for some time, and then ceased: directly after a figure emerged from the shade of the wood, and passed along the bank at a little distance before her.—It went swiftly, and her spirits were so overcome with awe, that, though she saw, she did not much observe it. This little occurrence deeply oppressed her mind, and when she retired to her own room, it was some time before she sunk to repose.—But this was of short duration, for one of the maids had fainted, and fallen against her door. When the girl had recovered her speech, she affirmed that in passing up the back staircase, she had seen an apparition on the second landing-place, which had vanished at the door of the apartments lately opened.

This last event raised such a terror in the servants, that many spoke of quitting the Castle, till Rovedo, laughing at their folly, proposed to watch for the ghost; and Henri and the Count willingly said they would accompany him. Rovedo, taking his sword and a lamp, they unlocked the north hall door, and proceeded through the suite of rooms till they came to the bed-room. After surveying the pall, and being told that the Marchioness died in that bed, the Count ordered some provisions, wine, and fuel, to be left with Rovedo, and then wishing him well through the night, they retired. Rovedo, having examined the apartments to see that no one was concealed, returned to the bed-room, kindled a fire, drew forth his provision, and when he had done, began to read a book of Provençal tales.[1] In the mean time, the Count and his party retired to rest for the night: while the former was undressing, he was astonished by the sounds of music and a fine voice in accompaniment.—The valet informed him it was the same music that came from the woods, and which no one could account for. Count Amant, the following morning knocked at the door of the north chamber, but received no answer: he then repaired to one opening nearly on the saloon, which, having forced, he entered through the saloon into the bed-room, followed by Henri, and a few of the most courageous servants. No trace of Rovedo appeared there, and the Count began to be seriously alarmed for his safety.—What made his disappearance extraordinary was, that all the doors were found to be bolted and locked on the inside, and there seemed no way by which he could have escaped or secreted himself. On the table was his sword, the lamp, the book, and the remains of a flask of wine he had been drinking. The Count and Henri, after looking every where for a secret way of getting out, gave over the search, and retired together to the Count's closet, whence Henri returned much depressed in his spirits. Poor Alise felt more than any one the loss of her Rovedo. In a week after his disappearance, M. La Fleur paid a visit to the Count, and renewed his suit to Emily. This measure determined Emily to return to the Convent; the reason of which she stated to be, that she might not encourage a hopeless passion in a man whom she highly esteemed. On the following evening the Abbess and sisters welcomed her again, and she was pleased to find herself once more in their tranquil society. The strange events at the Castle had reached the convent, and Emily was surprised to learn

[1] That is, tales from the Provençe region of southern France; such tales were characteristically associated with fanciful adventure. As Radcliffe herself explains in *Udolpho*, "The fictions of the Provençal writers, whether drawn from the Arabian legends, brought by the Saracens into Spain, or recounting the chivalric exploits performed by the crusaders, whom the Troubadours accompanied to the east, were generally splendid and always marvellous, both in scenery and incident..." (Volume IV, Chapter 6). Radcliffe takes this opportunity to tell her own "Provençal tale," inserting into her novel a chivalric tale of over 2,100 words, and featuring a genuine ghost.

from sister Anna, to whom she was more attached than the others, that they had a sister named Doria, whose conduct and manner, whenever the Castle was mentioned, shewed her to be somewhat deranged on that particular subject. The speeches of Doria seemed to fix fault on the late Marquis, and at the same time to feel a wound in her own conscience.

When the nuns had retired to rest, Emily repaired to the cell of Anna, who briefly related what she knew in the following words: "Sister Doria is of a noble family, whose name I shall not dishonour by revealing it.—She loved a poor gentleman, and her father bestowed her on a nobleman she did not like: hence she profaned the marriage vows; but her guilt was detected, and she would have fallen a sacrifice to her husband's vengeance, had not her father contrived means to convey her from his power. By what means he did this I never could learn: she was placed in this convent, and afterwards took the veil, while a report was circulated to the world that she was dead, and the father employed such means as induced the husband to believe she had fallen a victim to his jealousy." Emily was much affected by the similarity of this story to that of the Marchioness, the only difference in which seemed to be the certainty of the latter's death. "I cannot but remark," continued Anna, "the similarity of your features to the forlorn Doria's, whose place of refuge has been here about as many years as makes your age." "It was about that same period the Marchioness de Lormel died," said Emily, and she sunk into a reverie, from which she was aroused by the midnight bell sounding for prayers. Emily then returned to her chamber, and the nun went to the chapel. In the mean time, the Count Amant received a letter from the advocate at Avignon, advising Emily to assert her claim to the estates of her late aunt, as he had received intelligence from Venice that Androssi had died in prison, and Rodoni had been convicted and executed for assassination. The Count also received a letter from M. Lebas, stating that the only person, who could oppose Emily's claim at Thoulouse, was dead; and the term for which La Vallée had been let being nearly expired, he advised her in less than three weeks to make that chateau in her way from Thoulouse.

The Count having waited on Emily, declared that the tranquillity of his mind was so much interrupted by the events in the castle, that he and his daughter would accompany the Baron St. Foix to his chateau, and Emily invited the Count to visit her at La Vallée, as the chateau was at no great distance. On the receipt of another letter from Lebas, stating that La Vallée was at liberty, she set out for Thoulouse, attended by the unhappy Alise, and guarded by a servant of the Count's. During the journey, her mind was occupied by the scene, which reminded her at every step of Angereau, till she reached her own mansion. Having entered the large oak parlour, the common sitting room of Madame Androssi, she found a letter from Lebas, excusing his not meeting her from urgent business. Every thing here reminded her again of the absent Angereau, and being desirous of quitting Thoulouse, she immediately dispatched a part of the necessary business concerning the estate, according to the directions of M. Lebas.—This day was devoted entirely to business, and in the evening her spirits were so much strengthened, that she thought she could bear to visit the gardens where she had so often walked with Angereau. She therefore repaired to the terrace, and entered the pavilion, where she sat till the sun had set, thinking on his follies; and, recollecting the emphatic words of her father, "this young man has never been at Paris!" she exclaimed, "Ah! if he had had a mentor like my father, his generous nature had never fallen!" As she passed along the terrace in returning, she observed the figure of a man slowly winding among the trees, walking in a pensive attitude.—Alarmed, Emily fled to the house, and concealed from every one the knowledge of the mysterious wanderer, whom she fancied might have been Angereau.

The third day after this, Alise brought her intelligence that the gardens on the preceding night had been infested by a robber, whom the gardener had fired at, and wounded by the blood on the ground, but he had made his escape.—The shock of this event overcame Emily's fortitude, as she resolved the robber into the person of the melancholy Angereau. Having sent to all the neighbouring cottages to learn if a wounded gentleman had entered for relief, and hearing nothing to confirm her opinion, she resolved immediately to set off for La Vallée, where her friends proposed to visit her in two days. Emily departed early in the morning, and reached La Vallée about sun-set. Here she visited the haunts of her late father, and still felt that La Vallée was her happiest home.

The first business of Emily was to enquire out the residence of

Theresa, who lived in a collage provided by the generous Angereau, when M. Lebas turned her from the chateau. The joy of the good old creature was extreme, and the long stories she told of Angereau's visits to La Vallée, after Emily had left it, were highly pleasing to the latter. He had allowed quarterly money to Theresa, which had failed only in the last payment. This omission Emily could easily account for, and she now desired Theresa to hire some person to go to his steward to ask for her quarterage, and make enquiries concerning Angereau, which the old servant immediately set about doing.[1] The route of the Count lay over the Pyrenees, from the chateau of the Baron de St. Foix to La Vallée. Young St. Foix accompanied him; he was to be united to Lady Blanche on their return home. Having wandered out of their track, and a storm coming on, they descried a watch tower, to which their guide immediately proceeded with the mules. On drawing nearer, they perceived it was an extensive ruinated fortress, situated on the summit of a cliff. Having found a path to it, and considering that their own party was well armed they advanced to the gate, and knocking, a voice demanded who was there. The Count answered, some friends who had lost their way; on which the door was opened by a man in a hunter's dress, who was joined by several others; they pressed them to enter, and partake of such fare as they were about to sit down to. The Count then entered with his servants, and were conducted to a rude hall, round which four men in hunter's dresses were seated, and two dogs.

The Count commenced a conversation with them upon their seeming avocation, and presently after the horn sounded, and two men entered, armed with guns and pistols: one of them was in a faded uniform. Throwing down their knapsacks, they drew forth two or three brace of birds; but the Count thought the bags sounded as if they had metal in them. Shortly after, the party invited their guests to follow to the gallery; the long ruinous passages through which they went, accompanied with the rolling thunder, somewhat daunted them. The hunters led the way with a lamp; Blanche followed trembling.—As she passed on, her robe caught to a nail, and while she stopped to disengage it, the Count and St. Foix turned an

[1] The shift from Emily's meeting with Theresa to the story of the Count's journey is signalled by the beginning of a new chapter in *Udolpho*; the chapbook's combining of the two disparate events in a single paragraph is confusing, to say the least.

angle, and Blanche was left in darkness. She followed the way she thought they had taken, but it led to a chamber where four men were seated in deep conversation round a table. She looked with surprise on observing the soldier among them who had last entered, and who addressed his companions on the most easy way of murdering the travellers who had just taken refuge.

Blanche, who had listened to this conversation in agony, now endeavoured to fly, in doing which she stumbled, and alarmed the banditti, who rushed out, discovered the object of their alarm, and bore her into the room. They held a consultation what to do with her, but the first resolution they agreed on was to plunder her. While she was intreating them to pity, a distant noise was heard, and in the next moment a clashing of swords took place in the avenue leading to the chamber.—Three of them then rushed out, on being called by their comrades, and in a few seconds after St. Foix entered, pursued by several ruffians. Blanche sunk into the arms of the robber who detained her, and when she recovered, St. Foix lay at a little distance, covered with blood and speechless.—Calling loudly for assistance, a man flew into the chamber; it was Rovedo!—He was followed by the Count, with his sword reddened with blood, who pressed his daughter to his bosom, and then joined Rovedo in recovering St. Foix.—Having overcome and secured the banditti in a dungeon, they recommenced their journey, moving slowly on account of the wounds of St. Foix. The morning had now dawned, and when they had proceeded a few leagues, they stopped to refresh under some green pines, during which Rovedo related his adventures since leaving the chateau of Mount Blanc.

While these events were taking place, Theresa's messenger had returned from Angereau's brother, and she had sent notice to Emily to come to her cottage. It appeared that Angereau, when he quitted Paris for Thoulouse, and returned to his brother's, was very coldly received by him, soon after which he went away into Languedoc, and had not since been heard of. Emily was pacing the room in an agony of grief, when a voice that spoke without drew her attention. She listened, and turning her eyes to the door, the bright beams of the fire shone upon the features of Angereau! She sunk on the floor, and when she recovered beheld herself in his arms. He could only exclaim—"Emily!" while he silently watched her looks. Emily assumed a reserve in her manner, but the joy of old Theresa's heart disclosed all the anxieties her mistress had felt for his absence. Emily's request, however, that Angereau would quit the cottage, was delivered in such an impressive manner, that he no longer hesitated, but wishing she might be as happy as he was wretched, he departed. When Theresa informed her that the rain still continued, and that he bore his arm in a sling, her pity returned. The latter she had little doubt was occasioned by the gardener firing at him in the gardens of Thoulouse. which actually happened. He was on his way from that place to the chateau of a friend, and had called at Theresa's in his route.

The following day Rovedo arrived, to the great joy of Alise, at La Vallée: he brought letters from the Count to Emily, in which he informed her of his intention of repairing to Chateau le Blanc when young St. Foix was recovered, preparatory to the nuptials with his daughter, and requested Emily to be present. Emily's next pleasure was to hear of the manner in which Rovedo had escaped from the Chateau Le Blanc, which he detailed in the following words: "I had not sat long, after the Count had retired, when I was alarmed by a noise, and looking towards the bed, I fancied I saw a man's face within the dusky curtains. In the next moment the arras near the bed was slowly lifted, and four men entered from a door in the wall, and immediately seized me. The door and the passage they conveyed me through were cut in the solid wall, and might have escaped all observation. I was conducted to the vaults of the castle, whence we wound under subterraneous passages till we gained the sea shore; here I was put into a boat, and landed in Roussillon, and conveyed to the fortress of pirates, who had long made use of the north chambers of the Chateau le Blanc to deposit their contraband goods in, and thus had originated the idea of its being haunted. I overheard the plan to assassinate the Count and his party, but, by my timely intelligence, the scheme was frustrated, the villains defeated, and I liberated."

Emily now enquired if any of these men had ever entered the chamber alone, and was informed that one of them once was surprised by the sudden presence of two women; and, the better to hide himself, as he could not find the door readily, he got into the bed, where, by suddenly raising his head above the pall, he succeeded in frightening away the intruders. This explained in a natural way the cause of Emily's terror when she visited the chamber. Since the last

Count came, much of the noises heard had arisen from moving their goods: they took every opportunity of promoting a conviction that the castle was haunted, and when they made a captive of Rovedo, they considered the vaults of the castle as their own.

On the following day, the arrival of her friends revived the drooping Emily, and La Vallée became again the scene of social hospitality. After a week's stay, Emily departed with them for the Chateau Le Blanc, leaving Theresa in her old station of housekeeper. On their arrival, they found Henri and M. La Fleur there, in whose favour the Count again addressed Emily, but received the same discouragement as before. Emily took the first opportunity of visiting the convent, and there learned that the sister Doria was dying. At the gate of the convent stood a coach and horses, which had brought a Monsieur Benoit from Paris, to see the departing nun, at her request. As Doria had often, in her ravings, called on the name of Emily D'Orville, the abbess introduced her to her chamber. On seeing her, Doria exclaimed, "It is her very look! she possesses all that fascination which proved my destruction! Would you have retribution, it will soon be yours! How many years have passed since I last saw you!—My crime is but as yesterday!—Can tears and repentance wash out the foulness of murder!—Look there!—see she stalks along the room!—Why does she come to torment me now!—Hark! what groan was that!"—When the wild fit had subsided, she cast her melancholy eyes on Emily, and asked, notwithstanding her name was D'Orville, if she were not the daughter of the Marchioness de Lormel. Emily recollected that her father had requested to be buried in the vault of the Lormels, and she earnestly asked her reason for the question. Doria then produced a miniature, exactly resembling that found among her father's papers. "Keep this," said she, giving the picture to Emily, "for it is your right. How powerfully does the resemblance to you strike upon my conscience!"—She then directed a nun to a casket, whence she drew another picture, and presenting it to Emily said, "Behold the difference between what I was and what I now am!" The astonished eyes of Emily beheld the likeness of Signora Mirandini, which she had formerly seen in the castle of Gorgono, the lady who had disappeared in so mysterious a manner, and whom Androssi had been accused of murdering. Doria then proceeded, upon Emily saying that she had seen the original in the Appenine castle. "Learn, then, that

I am the Lady Mirandini, and you are daughter of the Marchioness de Lormel, who was attached to a gentleman of Gascony, when her father forced her to take the hand of the Marquis. Ill-fated unhappy woman! I tasted what is called the sweets of revenge.—I indulged the malignant passion of jealousy!—Alas! what scenes of suffering and horror did I transact at Chateau le Blanc!"—At this moment the veiled picture rushed upon the memory of Emily, and she exclaimed, "Your sudden departure from the castle—the west chamber—the veiled picture—murder!—Oh! speak in explanation!"—"Blood!" cried the dying nun, in a last convulsion, "there was no blood!—Nay, do not smile."—Here she became speechless. Emily then took her leave, and bent her way back to the castle, occupied by the important discovery made, and Lady Mirandini's assertion, that she was the daughter of the Marchioness de Lormel. She surmised that her father was the lover of the Marchioness, and that the papers destroyed related to the connexion; but the story sister Anna had told was evidently false, and, perhaps, fabricated by Doria to conceal the true one.

On the following morning Emily was told that Doria was no more. M. Benoit was less concerned at her death than he had been at her illness; perhaps he was consoled by having the major part of her property bequeathed to him, which might in some measure balance the distresses occasioned by an extravagant son. In speaking to La Fleur on the subject, he declared that he had been extricated from gaol by a fellow prisoner of the name of Angereau, who, on the first moment of liberation, had paid his debt, and procured his discharge. The conversation of M. Benoit clearly proved that Angereau had been the dupe of sharpers, and that, during the time he lay in prison till his brother released him, he had seen the folly of his conduct and his unworthiness of Emily. With what money he then had to spare, he went to the gaming-house, and hazarded it as a last stake, firmly resolving never more to adventure again. He was fortunate, and, with the money thus won, he released M. Benoit from prison, and restored him to his family; after which he left Paris for Esturviere. When La Fleur understood his rival was Angereau de Plessis, he acknowledged that they were friends, and henceforward he should resign all pretensions to Emily in favour of such a worthy man. The Count too found by M. Benoit that the stories of Angereau's follies were much exaggerated, and determined to oppose his union with Emily no longer.

A few days after the death of Signora Mirandini, the will was opened, and M. Benoit was found to possess her property except one third, which descended to the nearest surviving heir of the late Marchioness de Lormel, and Emily was the person. Mirandini di Gorgono was the heiress of the ancient house of Gorgono, in the territory of Venice. She possessed youth, beauty, and violent passions, at a time when the death of her father and mother left her to herself. Among her admirers was the late Marquis de Lormel, who solicited her hand in marriage. Before the nuptials, she retired to the castle of Gorgono, where her disposition becoming obvious to him, she became his only mistress. After a few weeks stay at the castle, he was called away to France, promising to return shortly, and celebrate the nuptials. Her relative, Androssi, soon after this addressed her, and was rejected. Tired with waiting for the absent Marquis, whom she warmly loved, and whose loss she every moment regretted, she set off for France, having heard a report that he had married there. On her arrival in Languedoc, she found it to be true; and then presented herself to the Marquis, whose firmness was not proof against her beauty and love. He had married from prudence, and esteemed his wife with only a lukewarm affection. The artful Italian, seeing her influence over the Marquis, contrived to convince him of his wife's infidelity, and hence in a rash moment he gave his consent to poison her. No sooner, however, was the deed done, than remorse and despair filled both their bosoms.

When the Marquis was informed that she was dying, he felt suddenly an assurance of her innocence, nor was the solemn assertion she made him in her last hour, capable of affording a stronger conviction of her blameless conduct.—In the first horrors of his mind the Marquis felt inclined to deliver up himself and the woman who had thus plunged him into guilt, into the hands of justice, but when the paroxysm of remorse had somewhat subsided, he changed this intention. He saw the Signora but once afterwards, and that was to tell her, that he would spare her life, on the condition only that she passed the rest of her days in prayer and penitence. Touched with horror at the unavailing crime she had committed, Signora Mirandini withdrew privately to the convent of St. Claire, and assumed the name of Doria. The Marquis, immediately after his wife's death, quitted Chateau le Blanc, to which he never returned; in vain did he endeavour to lose the sense of his sin in the tumult of war, or the gaieties of Paris: a deep dejection hung over him, which all the assiduities of his friends could not relieve, and he at length died with a keenness of conscience nearly equal to that which the partner of his guilt had suffered.

The physician, who had attended the unfortunate Marchioness, had been bribed to silence, and thus her death never reached correctly the ear of the Marchioness's father, who, most probably, would otherwise have prosecuted the iniquitous parties. Her death was particularly lamented by M. D'Orville, who was her brother. Many letters passed between the Marquis and him soon after the decease of his beloved sister; they related to the cause of her death, and were what he so ardently enjoined Emily to destroy. He could never hear her name mentioned without the deepest regret, and never let Emily know that he had such a relation,—a secret, which Madame Tissot, at his request, faithfully kept. Mirandini, on entering the convent, the better to conceal her real circumstances, had imposed a false story on Sister Anna.—Shortly a mixture of despair and melancholy seized upon her mind, and in these paroxysms she was indulged in her fancy of wandering at midnight round the convent, and singing to the music of her lute, on which she played excellently. Before she shewed symptoms of insanity she made a will, leaving a handsome sum to the convent, and dividing the rest between M. Benoit's wife, who was an Italian lady, and her relation, and the nearest survivor of the Marchioness. The resemblance between Emily and her aunt had been frequently observed by Signora Mirandini, and the bold assertion that followed, that Emily was the daughter of the Marchioness de Lormel, arose from a suspicion, that she was the issue of the favoured lover to whom the Marchioness had been so much attached before her marriage with the Marquis.—Of any murder, however, in Gorgono, Mirandini was innocent.—It may be remembered, that in a chamber of that castle, hung a black veiled picture, whose singular situation had excited Emily's curiosity, which, on lifting it, disclosed a view that overwhelmed her with horror. Instead of the picture she expected, within a recess of the wall lay a human figure, of cadaverous paleness, stretched at its length, and dressed in the habiliments of the grave.

What added to the horror of the spectacle was, that the face appeared partly decayed and disfigured by worms, which were visible on the features and hands.—The terrific sight prevented Emily from taking a second view; after the first glance, she had let the veil drop, and her terror prevented her ever after from renewing the suffering she then experienced. Had she dared to have proceeded to a second inspection, her fears and her conviction would have vanished together; she would then have perceived that the figure before her was not human, but formed of wax. The history of this figure, though somewhat extraordinary, is not inconsistent with that fierce severity which monkish superstition has sometimes inflicted on the bigotted and weak minded.—A former possessor of the Castle of Gorgono having committed some offence against the prerogative of the Church, in an insult offered to the holy friar of a neighbouring convent, was condemned to the penance of contemplating, during certain hours of the day, a waxen image, made to resemble a human body in the state to which it is reduced after death. This penance, serving as a memento of the condition at which he must arrive himself, had been designed to reprove the pride of the Marquis of Gorgono, which had formerly so much exasperated that of the Romish church.—He had not only superstitiously and religiously observed this penance himself, which the ignorance of that day believed was a free pardon for all sin, but he had made it a condition in his will, that his descendants should continue the image in its same position, placing over it only a black veil, on pain of forfeiting to the church a certain part of his domain, that they also might profit by the humiliating moral it conveyed.—The figure therefore had uninterruptedly retained its original station in the wall of the chamber; his descendants, however, had excused themselves from observing the penance to which the first lord had been enjoined.

The image was so dreadfully natural, that it is not surprising that Emily should have mistaken it for the object it represented; nor, since she had heard such an extraordinary account of the Lady Marchioness's sudden disappearance, and had also such an experimental knowledge of the turpitude of Androssi's heart, is it to be wondered at, that she should believe the figure to have been the murdered body of Lady Mirandini, and that he had been the contriver of her death, for the sake of getting a premature possession of the Castle, since he could not induce her to bestow her hand on him in marriage. The situation in which she had discovered it occasioned her at first much surprise and distress; but the vigilance, with which the doors of the chamber where it was deposited were afterwards secured, had induced her to believe that Androssi, not daring to confide the secret of her death to any person, had suffered her remains to moulder in this dark and gloomy chamber. The ceremony of the veil, however, and the circumstance of the door being left open when she entered, had occasioned her much wonder and doubt; but these were not able to overcome her suspicion of Androssi; and it was the dread of his terrible vengeance that had sealed her lips in silence, concerning the putrified body she thought she had seen in the western chamber.

In consequence of the late discoveries, Emily was distinguished by the Count and his family as the heiress of the house of De Lormel; and received, if possible, greater attention than had yet been shewn her. The Count's surprise, at the delay of an answer to the letter he had sent to Angereau at Estuviere, increased daily. The preparations for the approaching nuptials of Lady Blanche rather depressed than elevated the spirits of Emily, since it reminded her of the absent generous Angereau, whose heart, she feared, might have sunk under the despair and grief occasioned by her unkindness. The state of suspence, to which she believed herself condemned till she should return to La Vallée, appeared insupportable, and in such moments she would abruptly retire from the company, and endeavour to hide her feelings in the deep solitudes of the woods that overbrowed the beach.

One evening, having wandered to a favorite ruinated watch-tower, romantically situated on the sea-shore, she touched her lute to songs of gentle sadness, and sung till the remembrance of past times were too powerful for her heart, when her tears rendered her unable to proceed. She continued to indulge her melancholy reverie till she heard a footstep below at a little distance, and observed it was M. Benoit. After some time she again struck her lute, and sung her favorite air. As she paused between the stanzas, she heard a step ascending the staircase of the tower. In the next moment the door of the chamber opened, and a person entered, whose features were veiled in the solemnity of twilight, but his voice was too well known to be concealed: Emily started at the sound of her name ejaculated from the lips of Angereau, and sunk, overcome, upon her seat. Angereau, as he hung over her, deplored his rash impatience, which, on his arrival at the chateau, had induced him to seek Emily without sending previous notice. It was a considerable time before she recovered, but when she did, her manner was reserved, and she asked the motive for his breaking in upon her retirement. Angereau's countenance suddenly changed, and in an accent of despair he exclaimed, "I had been taught to hope for a different reception!—I thought you had known how cruelly my conduct has been misrepresented, and that the actions which you once thought me guilty of, I hold in as much contempt and abhorrence as yourself.—Can you be ignorant that the Count Amant has detected the slanders that have robbed me of your affection?"

Emily paused, and then, after a sigh, said, "Angereau, till this moment I was ignorant of all the circumstances you have mentioned.—The emotion I now suffer may convince you that I have not entirely forgotten, nor ceased to esteem, you. These are the first moments of joy I have known since I last saw you, and they repay me for all the anxiety I have felt for the honour and dignity of Angereau!" Angereau was unable to reply, but pressed her hand to his lips, while his tears falling on it, spoke a language superior to the power of words.

Emily, somewhat tranquillised, proposed returning to the chateau, where the Count welcomed him with the joy of pure benevolence, and solicited his forgiveness for the injustice he had done him. M. Benoit soon after joined the happy group, and he and Angereau were mutually rejoiced to meet. M. St. Foix was expected every hour at the chateau, and soon joined the party, which continued up till late hour, yielding to the delights of social friendship. The noble La Fleur did not throw any gloom by his presence, having withdrawn from the chateau to forget in absence the beauties and perfection he was yielding up to his friend Angereau. The marriages of Lady Blanche and Emily D'Orville were celebrated on the same day, and with all the ancient baronial magnificence. After gracing the festivities of Chateau le Blanc for some days, Angereau and his Lady took leave of their kind friends, and returned to La Vallée, where the faithful Theresa received them with unfeigned joy.

Soon after their return to La Vallée, the brother of Angereau came to congratulate him on his marriage, and pay his respects to Emily, with whose virtues and manners he was so well pleased, that he immediately resigned to him a part of his domains, the rest of which would descend to his brother on his decease. The estates at Thoulouse being disposed of, Emily purchased of M. Lebas the paternal domains of her late father. Having given Alise a marriage portion, she appointed her to the post of housekeeper, and made Rovedo her steward. The legacy which Signora Mirandini had bequeathed to Emily, she begged Angereau would permit her to resign in favour of M. Benoit. The Castle of Gorgono also descended to the wife of the latter, who was the nearest surviving relation of the house of that name.—Thus was affluence restored to this worthy family, which had been nearly ruined by a profligate son, and relieved by Angereau.—The latter settled at La Vallée, and the chateau became again the residence of benevolence and domestic happiness.

FINIS.

Appendix A: Compressing *Udolpho*

The Veiled Picture is, among other things, a marvel of literary economy, condensing Radcliffe's four-volume masterwork to a small bluebook of only 72 pages. As discussed in the Introduction, this remarkable compression is accomplished largely by the severe pruning of every textual detail not directly relevant to plot development. The following examples illustrate the extent of compression achieved by the redactor.

Example 1:

In the story of *The Veiled Picture/Udolpho*, Emily's father is sent by his physician to the south of France in order to recover his health. He grows steadily weaker as he and Emily travel, particularly after they take leave of Angereau/Valancourt, and in one especially remote area finds himself almost too weak to bear the motion of the carriage. Unable to find lodgings, Emily sets out from the carriage—leaving their driver, Michael, behind—to investigate music that appears to be coming from a chateau half-hidden in the woods. She does not find it, but does come across a group of benevolent peasants.

Here is how *The Veiled Picture* describes her attempt to locate help:

> "At the end of a long shadowy lane, Emily discovered a party of vintagers merry-making...."

Here is the same search for assistance as depicted in *Udolpho*:

> "... she stepped from the carriage in search of the chateau she had seen at a distance. It was a still moon-light night, and the music, which yet sounded on the air, directed her steps from the high road, up a shadowy lane, that led to the woods. Her mind was for some time so entirely occupied by anxiety and terror for her father, that she felt none for herself, till the deepening gloom of the overhanging foliage, which now wholly excluded the moon-light, and the wildness of the place, recalled her to a sense of her adventurous situation. The music had ceased, and she had no

guide but chance. For a moment she paused in terrified perplexity, till a sense of her father's condition again overcoming every consideration for herself, she proceeded. The lane terminated in the woods, but she looked round in vain for a house, or a human being, and as vainly listened for a sound to guide her. She hurried on, however, not knowing whither, avoiding the recesses of the woods, and endeavouring to keep along their margin, till a rude kind of avenue, which opened upon a moon-light spot, arrested her attention. The wildness of this avenue brought to her recollection the one leading to the turreted chateau, and she was inclined to believe, that this was a part of the same domain, and probably led to the same point. While she hesitated, whether to follow it or not, a sound of many voices in loud merriment burst upon her ear. It seemed not the laugh of cheerfulness, but of riot, and she stood appalled. While she paused, she heard a distant voice, calling from the way she had come, and, not doubting but it was that of Michael, her first impulse was to hasten back; but a second thought changed her purpose; she believed that nothing less than the last extremity could have prevailed with Michael to quit his mules, and fearing that her father was now dying, she rushed forward, with a feeble hope of obtaining assistance from the people in the woods. Her heart beat with fearful expectation, as she drew near the spot whence the voices issued, and she often startled when her steps disturbed the fallen leaves. The sounds led her towards the moon-light glade she had before noticed; at a little distance from which she stopped, and saw, between the boles of the trees, a small circular level of green turf, surrounded by the woods, on which appeared a group of figures. On drawing nearer, she distinguished these, by their dress, to be peasants, and perceived several cottages scattered round the edge of the woods, which waved loftily over this spot. While she gazed, and endeavoured to overcome the apprehensions that withheld her steps, several peasant girls came out of a cottage; music instantly struck up, and the dance began. It was the joyous music of the vintage! the same she had before heard upon the air. Her heart, occupied with terror for her father, could not feel the contrast, which this gay scene offered to her own distress; she stepped hastily forward towards a group of elder peasants, who were seated at the door of a cottage, and, having explained her situation, entreated their assistance."

Radcliffe's original demonstrates a mastery of the psychology of terror and anxiety as well as a master's touch in developing landscape impressions; her 547 words have been compressed to 15.

Example 2:

From *Udolpho*: Emily is on the verge of being forced to marry Count Morano when the marriage is suddenly postponed by the arrival of Montoni's friend, Orsino:

> An affair, however, soon after occurred, which somewhat called off Montoni's attention from Emily. The mysterious visits of Orsino were renewed with more frequency since the return of the former to Venice. There were others, also, besides Orsino, admitted to these midnight councils, and among them Cavigni and Verezzi. Montoni became more reserved and austere in his manner than ever; and Emily, if her own interests had not made her regardless of his, might have perceived, that something extraordinary was working in his mind.
>
> One night, on which a council was not held, Orsino came in great agitation of spirits, and dispatched his confidential servant to Montoni, who was at a Casino, desiring that he would return home immediately; but charging the servant not to mention his name. Montoni obeyed the summons, and, on meeting Orsino, was informed of the circumstances, that occasioned his visit and his visible alarm, with a part of which he was already acquainted.
>
> A Venetian nobleman, who had, on some late occasion, provoked the hatred of Orsino, had been way-laid and poniarded by hired assassins: and, as the murdered person was of the first connections, the Senate had taken up the affair. One of the assassins was now apprehended, who had confessed, that Orsino was his employer in the atrocious deed; and the latter, informed of his danger, had now come to Montoni to consult on the measures necessary to favour his escape. He knew, that, at this time, the officers of the police were upon the watch for him, all over the city; to leave it, at present, therefore, was impracticable, and Montoni consented to secrete him for a few days till the vigilance of justice should relax, and then to assist him in quitting Venice. He knew the danger he himself incurred by permitting Orsino to remain

> in his house, but such was the nature of his obligations to this man, that he did not think it prudent to refuse him an asylum.
>
> Such was the person whom Montoni had admitted to his confidence, and for whom he felt as much friendship as was compatible with his character.
>
> While Orsino remained concealed in his house, Montoni was unwilling to attract public observation by the nuptials of Count Morano; but this obstacle was, in a few days, overcome by the departure of his criminal visitor, and he then informed Emily, that her marriage was to be celebrated on the following morning.

Here is how *Veiled Picture* reduces those 407 words to 83:

> An affair now happened which delayed the marriage for a few days. Androssi's friend, Rodoni, had privately assassinated a nobleman, and the senate having taken up the business, one of the bravos, for the sake of the reward, had confessed his employer's name. Rodoni, therefore, flew to his friend, who secreted him till the energy of justice had relaxed, and he had effected his escape from Venice. On the next evening, Androssi informed Emily that she was to be married the following morning.

Appendix B: Contemporary Reviews of *The Mysteries of Udolpho*

British Critic 4 (August 1794): 110-21

We so seldom find, in a work of imagination, those qualities combined, which are necessary to its successful accomplishment, that when the event does happen, we distinguish it as a place of repose from our severer labours, and are happy to beguile the hours of weariness and chagrin beneath the shade which fancy spreads around. A tale, regularly told, neither offending probability by its extravagance, nor fatiguing by its want of vivacity or incident, has ever been esteemed among those labours of the mind which the critic cannot disdain to commend, nor genius to introduce, and when it is further embellished by the charms of good writing, is the vehicle of ingenuous sentiments, and inculcates the purest morality, it eminently takes the lead in that class of writings, which is professedly designed for entertainment.

Mrs. Radcliffe had before obtained considerable reputation, from the cultivation of this branch of literature, and we are happy that it has fallen to our province to record one of the best and most interesting of her works. . . .

The Mysteries of Udolpho have too much of the terrific: the sensibility is sometimes jaded, and curiosity in a manner worn out. The endeavour to explain supernatural appearances and incidents, by plain and simple facts, is not always happy. . . . With respect to the style, we have little further to remark, or to censure, it is uniformly animated, and, in general, sufficiently correct.—We have read the whole with satisfaction, and entertain no doubt of its being well received by the public.

Gentleman's Magazine, 64, Pt. 2 (Sept. 1794): 834

The former work of this lady had raised the attention of the publick to her abilities, of which the present has by no means lessened their opinion. We trust, however, we shall not be thought unkind or severe if we object to the too great frequency of landscape-painting; which, though it shows the extensiveness of her observation and invention, wearies the reader with its repetitions. The plot is admirably kept up; but perhaps the reader is held too long in suspence and the development brought on too hastily in the concluding volume.

Monthly Review, ns 15 (Nov. 1794): 278-83

If the merit of fictitious narratives may be estimated by their power of pleasing, Mrs. Radcliffe's romances will be entitled to rank highly in the scale of literary excellence. There are, we believe, few readers of novels who have not been delighted with her Romance of the Forest; and we incur little risque in predicting that the Mysteries of Udolpho will be perused with equal pleasure.

The works of this ingenious writer not only possess, in common with many other productions of the same class, the agreeable qualities of correctness of sentiment and elegance of style, but are also distinguished by a rich vein of invention, which supplies an endless variety of incidents to fill the imagination of the reader; by an admirable ingenuity of contrivance to awaken his curiosity, and to bind him in the chains of suspence; and by a vigour of conception and a delicacy of feeling which are capable of producing the strongest sympathetic emotions, whether of pity or terror. Both these passions are excited in the present romance, but chiefly the latter; and we admire the enchanting power with which the author at her pleasure seizes and detains them. We are no less pleased with the proofs of sound judgment, which appear in the selection of proper circumstances to produce a distinct and full exhibition, before the reader's fancy, both of persons and events; and, still more, in the care which has been taken to preserve his mind in one uniform tone of sentiment, by presenting to it a long continued train of scenes and incidents, which harmonize with each other. . . .

Another part of the merit of this novel must not be overlooked. The characters are drawn with uncommon distinctness, propriety, and boldness. Emily, the principal female character, being naturally possessed of delicate sensibility and warm affection, is early warned by her father against indulging the pride of fine feelings—(the romantic error of amiable minds)—and is taught that the strength of fortitude is more valuable than the grace of sensibility. Hence she acquires a habit of self command, which gives a mild dignity to her manners, and a steady firmness to her conduct. . . .

The numerous mysteries of the plot are fully disclosed in the conclusion, and the reader is perfectly satisfied at finding villainy punished, and steady virtue and persevering affection rewarded. If there be any part of the story which lies open to material objection, it is that which makes Valancourt, Emily's lover, fall into disgraceful indiscretions during her absence, and into a temporary alienation of affection. . . .

The embellishments of the work are highly finished. The descriptions are rich, glowing, and varied: they discover a vigorous imagination and an uncommon command of language; and many of them would furnish admirable subjects for the pencil of the painter. If the reader, in the eagerness of curiosity, should be tempted to pass over any of them for the sake of proceeding more rapidly with the story, he will do both himself and the author injustice. They recur, however, too frequently; and, consequently, a similarity of expression is often perceptible. . . .

***Analytical Review* 19 (June 1794): 140-145.**

Mrs. Radcliffe has already afforded the town so much entertainment by her former works, particularly the Romance of the Forest, that our expectations were naturally raised, on the publication of the present. We are happy in confessing, that the pleasure derived from it has not barely answered our expectations, but far surpassed them. It is not enough to say, that the Mysteries of Udolpho is a pretty, or an agreeable romance. The design has ingenuity and contrivance; the style is correct and elegant; the descriptions are chaste and magnificent; and the whole work is calculated to give the author a distinguished place among fine writers. . . .

The fourth volume opens with a scene, in which the emotions of love, pity, grief, and anguish, are described with inimitable delicacy, when count [*sic*] de Villefort, at whose chateau Emily is, discovers to Emily the profligate conduct of Valancourt, which is confirmed by his own acknowledgment. . . . the history closes so as to leave virtue crowned with happiness, and vice in deserved punishment.

The plot of this story is so artfully contrived, and the incidents so surprising, as to make it perfectly answer to the genius of a romance. . .

Though we cannot sufficiently admire the descriptive powers of our fair author, justice obliges us to observe, that her descriptions sometimes partake too much of uniformity, and those of the evening particularly are much too frequent. In language, however, Mrs. R. is never defective, and what might have been expected in a work of this kind, never redundant, or falsely luxuriant. . . .

Thus far we have considered the merit of Mrs. R. as a writer of prose; but it would be injustice, to pass unnoticed the poetical productions interspersed in these volumes: many of the little pieces have very great merit; but some abound too much with monosyllables, which give feebleness to poetry. As Mrs. R. will, no doubt, appear again before the public as a writer, and perhaps of verse, as well as prose, her good taste will, we trust, correct this defect. She has given ample proof of her poetical talents. . . .

The Critical Review, ns vol.14 (August 1794), pp. 361-72.

[*This review has long been attributed to Samuel Taylor Coleridge, although scholarship since 1951 has established that attribution as incorrect.*]

> Thine too these golden keys, immortal boy!
> This can unlock the gates of joy,
> Of horror, that and thrilling fears,
> Or ope the sacred source of sympathetic tears.[1]

Such were the presents of the Muse to the infant Shakespeare, and though perhaps to no other mortal has she been so lavish of her gifts, the keys referring to the third line Mrs. Radcliffe must be allowed to be completely in possession of. This, all who have read the *Romance of the Forest* will willingly bear witness to. Nor does the present production require the name of its author to ascertain that it comes from the same hand. The same powers of description are displayed, the same predilection is discovered for the wonderful and the gloomy—the same mysterious terrors are continually exciting in the mind the idea of a supernatural appearance, keeping us, as it were, upon the very edge and confines of the world of spirits, and yet are ingeniously explained by familiar causes; curiosity is kept upon the stretch from page to page, and from volume to volume, and the secret, which the reader thinks himself every instant on the point of penetrating, flies like a phantom before him, and eludes his eagerness till the very last moment of protracted expectation. This art of escaping the guesses of the reader has been improved and brought to perfection along with the reader's sagacity; just as the various inventions of locks, bolts, and

---

[1] From Thomas Gray's "The Progress of Poesy," ll. 91-94.

private drawers, in order to secure, fasten, and hide, have always kept pace with the ingenuity of the pickpocket and house-breaker, whose profession is to unlock, unfasten, and lay open what you have taken so much pains to conceal. In this contest of curiosity on one side, and invention on the other, Mrs. Radcliffe has certainly the advantage. She delights in concealing her plan with the most artificial contrivance, and seems to amuse herself with saying, at every turn and doubling of the story, "Now you think you have me, but I shall take care to disappoint you." This method is, however, liable to the following inconvenience, that in the search of what is new, an author is apt to forget what is natural; and, in rejecting the more obvious conclusions, to take those which are less satisfactory. The trite and the extravagant are the Scylla and Charybdis of writers who deal in fiction. With regard to the work before us, while we acknowledge the extraordinary powers of Mrs. Radcliffe, some readers will be inclined to doubt whether they have been exerted in the present work with equal effect as in the *Romance of the Forest*. Four volumes cannot depend entirely on terrific incidents and intricacy of story. They require character, unity of design, a delineation of the scenes of real life, and the variety of well supported contrast. *The Mysteries of Udolpho* are indeed relieved by much elegant description and picturesque scenery; but in the descriptions there is too much of sameness: the pine and the larch tree wave, and the full moon pours its lustre through almost every chapter. Curiosity is raised oftener than it is gratified; or rather, it is raised so high that no adequate gratification can be given it; the interest is completely dissolved when once the adventure is finished, and the reader, when he is got to the end of the work, looks about in vain for the spell which had bound him so strongly to it. There are other little defects, which impartiality obliges us to notice. The manners do not sufficiently correspond with the æra the author has chosen; which is the latter end of the sixteenth century. There is, perhaps, no direct anachronism, but the style of accomplishments given to the heroine, a country young lady, brought up on the banks of the Garonne; the mention of botany; of little circles of infidelity, &c. give so much the air of modern manners, as is not counter-balanced by Gothic arches and antique furniture. It is possible that the manners of different ages may not differ so much as we are apt to imagine, and more than probable that we are generally wrong when we attempt to delineate any but our own; but there is at least a style of manners which our imagination has appropriated to each period, and which, like the costume of theatrical dress, is not departed from without hurting the feelings. The character of Annette, a talkative waiting-maid, is much worn, and that of the aunt, madame Cheron, is too low and selfish to excite any degree of interest, or justify the dangers her niece exposes herself to for her sake. . . .

If, in consequence of the criticisms impartiality has obliged us to make upon this novel, the author should feel disposed to ask us, Who will write a better? we boldly answer her, "Yourself"; when no longer disposed to sacrifice excellence to quantity, and lengthen out a story for the sake of filling an additional volume.

[*The following "addendum" to the above review appeared a month later:*]

CORRESPONDENCE — *Mysteries of Udolpho*

We have received a remonstrance on this subject; and can only say that we are sorry and surprised that any reader should so far mistake the object and intention of our critique on that ingenious performance; we, however, rejoice in the opportunity which is thus afforded us of explaining our sentiments, which we doubt not will be to the satisfaction of all parties.

It never could be our intention to depreciate the genius of Mrs. Radcliffe; for if our Correspondent will reexamine the introductory sentences of the Review in question, he will find such a compliment paid to the powers of her imagination as we seldom condescend to pay to any writer whatever.

It could not be our intention to speak slightingly of a work which all must admire, and which we have no hesitation in pronouncing "the most interesting novel in the English language." If such indeed had been our view, the very specimen which we selected would have completely refuted our decision.

But, while we cheerfully give to literary excellence its full tribute of praise, we must be allowed to point out whatever appears faulty in the most unexceptionable productions; and the more eminent the writer, the more pressing is our duty to guard against those faults which are concealed from common eyes under an accumulation of beauties.

It does not at all destroy the merit of *Udolpho* to say that it is not perfect. . . .

Appendix C: Contemporary Reactions to Radcliffe

Matthew Gregory Lewis[1]

[Lewis (1775-1818) was only nineteen when he wrote what immediately became the most notorious of Gothic novels, *The Monk* (1796); the story of a virtuous monk who succumbs to lust, rapes and murders his sister, and is finally claimed by Satan raised eyebrows and moral concerns from the moment it was published, and Lewis's election to Parliament only added to the scandal. (So troubled was Lewis by early reaction to his novel that he edited out many of the most salacious passages for subsequent editions.) Lewis went on to have considerable success as a Gothic dramatist, although he abandoned literature as a career when he inherited his family's sugar plantations in the West Indies.]

I have again taken up my romance [*The Monk*]; and perhaps by this time ten years, I may make shift to finish it fit for throwing it into the fire. I was induced to go on with it by reading the "Mysteries of Udolpho," which is, in my opinion, one of the most interesting books that has ever been published. I would advise you to read it by all means; but I must warn you, that it is not very entertaining till St. Aubyn's [*sic*] death. His travels, to my mind, are uncommonly dull, and I wish heartily that they had been left out, and something substituted in their room. I am sure you will be particularly interested by the part, when Emily returns home after her father's death: and when you read it, tell me whether you think there is any resemblance between the character given of Montoni, in the seventeenth chapter of the second volume, and my own. I confess that it struck me; and as he is the villain of the tale, I did not feel much flattered by the likeness.

Anna Lætitia Barbauld[2]

[Barbauld (1743-1825) was an influential writer, poet, and critic in the

[1] Letter to his mother dated 18 May 1794. *The Life and Correspondence of M.G. Lewis.* 2 vols. London: Colburn, 1839. I: 122-24.

[2] "Mrs. Radcliffe." Introductory Preface. *The British Novelists.* 50 vols. London: Rivington [et al.], 1810. 43: i-viii.

Romantic period. Many of her works were instructional and devotional works for children; she and her husband also ran a successful boarding school. Barbauld, of Dissenting background, was also a strong advocate for abolition and personal freedoms. She edited the influential 50-volume edition of *The British Novelists* in 1810.]

Though every production which is good in its kind entitles the author to praise, a greater distinction is due to those which stand at the head of a class; and such are undoubtedly the novels of Mrs. Radcliffe,—which exhibit a genius of no common stamp. She seems to scorn to move those passions which form the interest of common novels: she alarms the soul with terror; agitates it with suspense, prolonged and wrought up to the most intense feeling, by mysterious hints and obscure intimations of unseen danger. The scenery of her tales is in "time shook towers," vast uninhabited castles, winding stair-cases, long echoing aisles; or, if abroad, lonely heaths, gloomy forests, and abrupt precipices, the haunt of banditti;—the canvas and the figures of Salvator Rosa. Her living characters correspond to the scenery:—their wicked projects are dark, singular, atrocious. They are not of English growth; their guilt is tinged with a darker hue than that of the bad and profligate characters we see in the world about us; they seem almost to belong to an unearthly sphere of powerful mischief. But to the terror produced by the machinations of guilt, and the perception of danger, this writer has had the art to unite another, and possibly a stronger feeling. There is, perhaps, in every breast at all susceptible of the influence of imagination, the germ of a certain superstitious dread of the world unknown, which easily suggests the ideas of commerce with it. Solitude, darkness, low-whispered sounds, obscure glimpses of objects, flitting forms, tend to raise in the mind that thrilling, mysterious terror, which has for its object the "powers unseen and mightier far than we." But these ideas are suggested only; for it is the peculiar management of this author, that, though she gives, as it were, a glimpse of the world of terrible shadows, she yet stops short of any thing really supernatural: for all the strange and alarming circumstances brought forward in the narrative are explained in the winding up of the story by natural causes; but in the mean time the reader has felt their full impression.

Samuel Taylor Coleridge[1]

[One of the most important cultural figures of British Romanticism, Coleridge (1772-1834) was a poet, lecturer, moralist, essayist, and critic. He helped William Wordsworth inaugurate a poetic "revolution" with the joint publication of *Lyrical Ballads* in 1798, and was associated, in the public mind, with the Gothic largely on the basis of two poems: "The Rime of the Ancient Mariner" and "Christabel." While appreciate of the imaginative value of the supernatural, Coleridge, as the following excerpt from a letter to Wordsworth shows, had little patience with a literary genre that struck him as dominated by works of little moral or artistic value.]

I amused myself a day or two ago on reading a Romance in Mrs. Radcliff's [*sic*] style with making out a scheme, which was to serve for all romances a priori—only varying the proportions—A Baron or Baroness ignorant of their Birth, and in some dependent situation—Castle—on a Rock—a Sepulchre—at some distance from the Rock—Deserted Rooms—Underground Passages—Pictures—A ghost, so believed—or—a written record—blood on it!—A wonderful Cut throat—&c. &c. &c. . . .

John Keats

[The English poet John Keats (1795-1821) never referred to Radcliffe in his poetry, but his letters—widely regarded as among the most fascinating in British literary history—mention her twice. The first and most substantial mention is in a letter to Keats's friend J. H. Reynolds, dated 14 March 1818; it recognizes the powerful association of Radcliffe with sublime natural settings:][2]

> so we look upon a brook in these parts as you look upon a dash[3] in your Country—there must be something to support

[1] Letter to William Wordsworth (Oct. 1810). *Collected Letters of Samuel Taylor Coleridge.* Ed. Earl Leslie Griggs. 4 vols. (Oxford: Clarendon Press, 1956) III, 290-96.

[2] From *John Keats: A Critical Edition of the Major Works*. ed. Elizabeth Cook. New York: Oxford University Press, 1990, p. 384.

[3] "a splash; a sudden heavy fall of rain" (OED)

> this, aye fog, hail, snow rain—Mist—blanketing up three parts of the year—. . . . I am going among Scenery whence I intend to tip you the Damosel Radcliffe—I'll cavern you, and grotto you, and waterfall you, and wood you, and water you, and immense-rock you, and tremendous sound you, and solitude you. I'll make a lodgment on your glacis[1] by a row of Pines, and storm your covered way with bramble Bushes.

[The second mention is in a letter to his brother George and his wife Georgiana; the letter was written from 14 February to 3 May 1819:][2]

> Sunday Morn Feby 14th
>
> My dear Brother and Sister —
>
> I am still at Wentworth Place . . . . I was nearly a fortnight at Mr. John Snook's and a few days at old Mr. Dilke's. Nothing worth speaking of happened at either place. I took down some of the thin paper and wrote on it a little Poem call'd "St. Agnes Eve"—which you shall have as it is when I have finished the blank part of the rest for you . . .
> In my next Packet as this is one by the way, I shall send you the Pot of Basil, St Agnes eve, and if I should have finished it a little thing called the 'eve of St Mark'; you see what fine mother Radcliff names I have - it is not my fault - I did not search for them . . . .

The poems Keats refers to here ("The Eve of St. Mark" is unfinished) are among his works featuring ghosts, superstition, magic or fantasy, or some combination thereof. That Radcliffe is familiarly (and, perhaps, ironically) referred to as "Mother Radcliff" is further evidence of how inextricably her name had become linked with the Gothic; her name was almost a shorthand reference to the genre and its conventions.

---

[1] lodgment: a place of lodging; glacis: a gentle slope or incline

[2] From *Selected Poems and Letters* by John Keats, ed. Douglas Bush. Boston: Houghton Mifflin, 1959, p. 283.

Jane Austen

[The British novelist (1775-1817) best known for *Pride and Prejudice* also wrote, in 1798-9, a delightful Gothic parody, ultimately titled, when it was finally published in 1818, *Northanger Abbey*. Austen clearly knew her Gothic fiction, a fact evident not only in her masterful lampooning of Gothic conventions but in her mentions of various Gothic novels so obscure that for a century it was believed she had simply invented the titles. Yet it is *Udolpho* which holds pride of place, being given more attention in *Northanger Abbey* than any other Gothic fiction. The following exchange takes place between the innocent and impressionable Catherine, the heroine of the novel, and her worldly new friend, Isabella:]

> "But, my dearest Catherine, what have you been doing with yourself all this morning? Have you gone on with Udolpho?"
>
> "Yes, I have been reading it ever since I woke; and I am got to the black veil."
>
> "Are you, indeed? How delightful! Oh! I would not tell you what is behind the black veil for the world! Are not you wild to know?"
>
> "Oh! Yes, quite; what can it be? But do not tell me—I would not be told upon any account. I know it must be a skeleton, I am sure it is Laurentina's skeleton.[1] Oh! I am delighted with the book! I should like to spend my whole life in reading it. I assure you, if it had not been to meet you, I would not have come away from it for all the world."
>
> "Dear creature! How much I am obliged to you; and when you have finished Udolpho, we will read the Italian together; and I have made out a list of ten or twelve more of the same kind for you."
>
> "Have you, indeed! How glad I am! What are they all?"
>
> "I will read you their names directly; here they are, in my pocketbook. Castle of Wolfenbach, Clermont, Mysterious Warnings, Necromancer of the Black Forest, Midnight Bell,

---

[1] "Laurentina" is of course an error for "Laurentini."

Orphan of the Rhine, and Horrid Mysteries.[1] Those will last us some time."

"Yes, pretty well; but are they all horrid, are you sure they are all horrid?"

"Yes, quite sure; for a particular friend of mine, a Miss Andrews, a sweet girl, one of the sweetest creatures in the world, has read every one of them."

[Catherine and Isabella here exchange remarks on matters of flirtation; Catherine continues the conversation:]

". . . while I have Udolpho to read, I feel as if nobody could make me miserable. Oh! The dreadful black veil! My dear Isabella, I am sure there must be Laurentina's skeleton behind it."

"It is so odd to me, that you should never have read Udolpho before; but I suppose Mrs. Morland objects to novels."

"No, she does not. She very often reads Sir Charles Grandison[2] herself; but new books do not fall in our way."

"Sir Charles Grandison! That is an amazing horrid book, is it not? I remember Miss Andrews could not get through the first volume."

"It is not like Udolpho at all; but yet I think it is very entertaining."

"Do you indeed! You surprise me; I thought it had not been readable."

[In the following passage Catherine is conversing with John Thorpe, the ignorant and boorish brother of her new friend Isabella; the fact he does not know *The Mysteries of Udolpho* was authored by Ann Radcliffe is a clear indication of his cultural and intellectual deficiency.]

"Have you ever read Udolpho, Mr. Thorpe?"

"Udolpho! Oh, Lord! Not I; I never read novels; I have something else to do."

---

[1] These are the so-called "Northanger Novels" which, it was long (and erroneously) thought, were products of Austen's imagination.

[2] *Sir Charles Grandison* (1753) by Samuel Richardson, author of *Pamela* and *Clarissa*, all three of which were popular 18th century novels of morality and virtue.

Catherine, humbled and ashamed, was going to apologise for her question, but he prevented her by saying, "Novels are all so full of nonsense and stuff; there has not been a tolerably decent one come out since Tom Jones,[1] except The Monk; I read that t'other day; but as for all the others, they are the stupidest things in creation."

"I think you must like Udolpho, if you were to read it; it is so very interesting."

"Not I, faith! No, if I read any, it shall be Mrs. Radcliffe's; her novels are amusing enough; they are worth reading; some fun and nature in them."

"Udolpho was written by Mrs. Radcliffe," said Catherine, with some hesitation, from the fear of mortifying him.

"No sure; was it? Aye, I remember, so it was; I was thinking of that other stupid book, written by that woman they make such a fuss about, she who married the French emigrant."

"I suppose you mean Camilla?"[2]

"Yes, that's the book; such unnatural stuff! An old man playing at see-saw, I took up the first volume once and looked it over, but I soon found it would not do; indeed I guessed what sort of stuff it must be before I saw it: as soon as I heard she had married an emigrant, I was sure I should never be able to get through it."

Sir Walter Scott[3]

[Scott (1771-1832) was one of the most popular poets of the Romantic period prior to Lord Byron; once his poetic fame was eclipsed by that

---

[1] *Tom Jones* (1729) by Henry Fielding (1707-1754) is a comic novel of maturation, identity, and morality; it is more or less diametrically opposed to Matthew Lewis's *The Monk* (1796), which is packed with salacious, sensationalist, and even erotic elements. That John Thorpe would essentially equate these two novels is further evidence of his cultural cluelessness.

[2] *Camilla; or, A Picture of Youth* (1796) is by the British novelist and playwright Fanny Burney (1752-1840), who did indeed marry a French military officer and lived in France from 1802 to 1812. Burney was a close friend, coincidentally, of Hester Lynch Piozzi, whose travel narrative so strongly influenced Radcliffe. *Camilla* is directly influenced by *Udolpho* in its portrayals of powerful emotional states and psychological pressure.

[3] From *Lives of the Eminent Novelists and Dramatists*, London: Warne, 1887, pp. 551-578.

of Byron, Scott turned to novel writing, and helped create the historical novel with such landmark works as *Ivanhoe* and *Waverley*, among many others. Scott was also a prolific critic and editor.]

But although undoubtedly the talents of Mrs. Radcliffe, in the important point of drawing and finishing the characters of her narrative, were greatly improved since her earlier attempts, and manifested sufficient power to raise her far above the common crowd of novelists, this was not the department of art on which her popularity rested. The public were chiefly aroused, or rather fascinated, by the wonderful conduct of a story, in which the author so successfully called out the feelings of mystery and of awe, while chapter after chapter, and incident after incident, maintained the thrilling attraction of awakened curiosity and suspended interest. Of these, every reader felt the force, from the sage in his study, to the family group in middle life, which assembles round the evening taper, to seek a solace from the toils of ordinary existence by an excursion into the regions of imagination. The tale was the more striking, because varied and relieved by descriptions of the ruined mansion, and the forest with which it is surrounded, under so many different points of view, now pleasing and serene, now gloomy, now terrible—scenes which could only have been drawn by one to whom nature had given the eye of a painter, with the spirit of a poet.

In 1793, Mrs. Radcliffe had the advantage of visiting the scenery of the Rhine,[1] and although we are not positive of the fact, we are strongly inclined to suppose, that *The Mysteries of Udolpho* were written, or at least corrected, after the date of this journey; for the mouldering castles of the robber-chivalry of Germany, situated on the wild and romantic banks of that celebrated stream, seem to have given a bolder flight to her imagination, and a more glowing character to her colouring, than are exhibited in *The Romance of the Forest*. . . .

Much was of course expected from Mrs. Radcliffe's next effort, and the booksellers felt themselves authorized in offering what was then considered as an unprecedented sum, £500, for *The Mysteries of Udolpho*. It often happens, that a writer's previous reputation proves the greatest enemy which, in a second attempt upon public favour, he has to encounter. Exaggerated expectations are excited and circulated, and criticism, which had been seduced into former appro-

[1] Scott errs in supposing that Radcliffe had traveled to the Continent prior to the writing of *Udolpho*.

bation by the pleasure of surprise, now stands awakened and alert to pounce upon every failing. Mrs. Radcliffe's popularity, however, stood the test, and was heightened rather than diminished by *The Mysteries of Udolpho.* The very name was fascinating; and the public, who rushed upon it with all the eagerness of curiosity, rose from it with unsated appetite. When a family was numerous, the volumes always flew, and were sometimes torn, from hand to hand; and the complaints of those whose studies were thus interrupted, were a general tribute to the genius of the author. Another might be found of a different and higher description, in the dwelling of the lonely invalid, or unregarded votary of celibacy, who was bewitched away from a sense of solitude, of indisposition, of the neglect of the world, or of secret sorrow, by the potent charm of this mighty enchantress. Perhaps the perusal of such works may, without injustice, be compared with the use of opiates, baneful, when habitually and constantly resorted to, but of most blessed power in those moments of pain and of languor, when the whole head is sore, and the whole heart sick. If those who rail indiscriminately at this species of composition, were to consider the quantity of actual pleasure which it produces, and the much greater proportion of real sorrow and distress which it alleviates, their philanthropy ought to moderate their critical pride, or religious intolerance. . . .

The materials of these celebrated romances, and the means employed in conducting the narrative, are all selected with a view to the author's primary object, of moving the reader by ideas of impending danger, hidden guilt, supernatural visitings—by all that is terrible, in short, combined with much that is wonderful. . . .

In working upon the sensations of natural and superstitious fear, Mrs. Radcliffe has made much use of obscurity and suspense, the most fertile source, perhaps, of sublime emotion; for there are few dangers that do not become familiar to the firm mind, if they are presented to consideration as certainties, and in all their open and declared character; whilst, on the other hand, the bravest have shrunk from the dark and the doubtful. To break off the narrative, when it seemed at the point of becoming most interesting—to extinguish a lamp, just when a parchment containing some hideous secret ought to have been read—to exhibit shadowy forms and half-heard sounds of woe, are resources which Mrs. Radcliffe has employed with more effect than any other writer of romance. It must be confessed, that in order to bring about these situations, some art or contrivance, on the part of the author, is rather too visible. Her heroines voluntarily expose themselves to situations, which in nature a lonely female would certainly have avoided. They are too apt to choose the midnight hour for investigating the mysteries of a deserted chamber or secret passage, and generally are only supplied with an expiring lamp, when about to read the most interesting documents. The simplicity of the tale is thus somewhat injured—it is as if we witnessed a dressing up of the very phantom by which we are to be startled; and the imperfection, though redeemed by many beauties, did not escape the censure of criticism.

A principal characteristic of Mrs. Radcliffe's romances, is the rule which the author imposed upon herself, that all the circumstances of her narrative, however mysterious, and apparently superhuman, were to be accounted for on natural principles, at the winding up of the story. It must be allowed, that this has not been done with uniform success, and that the author has been occasionally more successful in exciting interest and apprehension, than in giving either interest or dignity of explanation to the means she has made use of.

Appendix D: Gothic Fiction/Gothic Architecture

As a glance at any list of Gothic titles will reveal, the role played by various architectural constructs (castles and abbeys, particularly) was prominent in the tradition, beginning with the work commonly identified as the first Gothic novel, Horace Walpole's *The Castle of Otranto* (1764).

The castle, being the dominant architectural space of early Gothics, is iconic for the genre in the minds of many readers, and its various symbolic possibilities form one of the staples of Gothic criticism and scholarship. But the role of the castle in Gothic fiction points to a pair of common questions: why is Gothic fiction "Gothic?" and what does it have to do with "Gothic" architecture?

One answer suffices for both.

Gothic architecture (generally held to be practiced from approximately 1150-1475, although there is considerable disagreement as to dates and definitions) was given its label by Renaissance artists, who found the vast, dark spaces of the typical cathedrals of the period—the most famous example being the Cathedral of Notre Dame in Paris—to be gloomy, melancholy places that unnecessarily complicated the classical beauties of Greek and Roman architectural principles. (To the builders of such works, and to modern architectural historians, much the opposite is true; Gothic architecture is in fact typically defined not only by its pointed arches and flying buttresses but by the almost transcendent sense of contained space and powerful vertical thrust embodied in comparatively slender walls and columns of soaring stone.) To such buildings the label "Gothic" was applied, alluding to the various Germanic peoples of Northern Europe who invaded parts of the Roman Empire in that Empire's waning years. The "Goths" ceased to exist centuries before the architectural style that still bears their name came into being, but the label was thought appropriate by those who applied it, for to the Renaissance mind "Goth" meant all that was barbaric, crude, and antithetical to the cultural values and glories of classicism. When Gothic fiction appeared in the later decades of the eighteenth century, the same technique and term was applied: Gothic fiction was "Gothic" because its overt supernaturalism and unrestrained emotionalism was crude and barbaric compared to the neo-classical formality and elegant restraint embodied in the works of Alexander Pope, John Dryden, and others. Yet the disparagement value of the term quickly dissipated as writers and readers embraced "Gothic" fiction, and the term quickly came to be a valued, and much over-used, marketing tool.

Appendix E: The Sublime

Stated simply, "the sublime" is that aesthetic category denoting nature's most powerful aspects and their effects upon the perceiving mind: storms at sea, towering mountains, natural disasters that do not directly threaten us—these speak of the vast power of nature, of energies and potentialities beyond human grasp, and in their power to move us, to elicit our terror or draw forth a sense of dread or our own cosmic insignificance, they are the most obvious manifestations of the sublime.

Radcliffe, like most educated people of her time, was deeply interested in the sublime and related aesthetic concepts, such as the picturesque and the beautiful, which were the subject of considerable scrutiny and vigorous debate in the eighteenth century. While the origins of "the sublime" lie in the rhetorical theories attributed to the Greek writer and philosopher Longinus (c. 213-273), who was concerned primarily with the power of language to move an audience, the sublime became a potent and contentious element of Western cultural debate only when translated into French, in 1674, by the poet Nicolas Boileau-Despréaux (1636-1711) and then engaged and adapted by various English writers, who sought to turn the sublime's innate fascination with human psychology—the "mechanics" of awe, in a sense—to spiritual and intellectual purposes. One of the first English writers to extend the idea of the sublime into the realm of aesthetics was John Dennis, who in *The Grounds of Criticism in Poetry* (1704) found the most powerful agents of sublimity were "Religious Ideas," specifically because of their ability to generate "Enthusiastick Terrour."[1] What Dennis and like-minded critics sought to do, in short, was to determine the ability of various ideas and objects to so impress the mind with intimations of divine power that the mind would be impelled toward God. When we are told, in *Udolpho*, that

> It was one of Emily's earliest pleasures to ramble among the scenes of nature; nor was it in the soft and glowing landscape that she most delighted; she loved more the wild wood-walks, that skirted the mountain; and still more the mountain's stupendous recesses, where the silence and grandeur of solitude impressed a sacred awe upon her heart, and lifted her thoughts to the GOD OF HEAVEN AND EARTH

---

[1] *The Grounds of Criticism in Poetry*. 1704. (Menston, England: Scolar, 1971): 76.

we are encountering an almost textbook instance of the religious sublime envisioned by Dennis and his followers. As explained by one scholar of sublimity, "The sublime is not created by man's ratiocinative processes but rather serves to signal their limitations: it occurs at the moment when man is overwhelmed by feelings of awe, wonder and terror on confronting aspects of the universe which go beyond his comprehension and which simultaneously reveal the grandeur of God and his own limited place in the divine scheme of things."[1] While Radcliffe's debt to the more secular sublime (discussed immediately below) has been well established,[2] her use of a more religiously informed sublime, such as in the passage just above, demonstrates her grasp and mastery of this aspect of aesthetics.

By the later years of the eighteenth century the sublime had begun to evolve in response to shifting cultural parameters. Long dominated by religious interpretations, the sublime began to reflect a growing interest in human emotion and psychology in a more secular context. One of the most influential texts in this development was Edmund Burke's *A Philosophical Enquiry into the Origin of our Ideas of the Sublime and the Beautiful* (2nd ed. 1759), which sought not a religious basis for the sublime, but a physiological and psychological one. For Burke, himself influenced by the empiricist theories of the British philosopher John Locke (1632-1704), the sublime was best understood as the numbing impact upon the mind of the observer, an impact with its roots in the pre-rational and with effects manifesting in a "suspension" so dramatic it verges on horror:

> The passion caused by the great and sublime in *nature*, when those causes operate most powerfully, is Astonishment; and astonishment is that state of the soul, in which all its motions are suspended, with some degree of horror. In this case the mind is so entirely filled with its object, that it cannot entertain any other, nor by consequence reason on that object which employs it. Hence arises the great power of the sub-

[1] David Morse, *Romanticism: A Structural Analysis* (Totowa, NJ: Barnes & Noble, 1982): 140.

[2] See Malcolm Ware, *Sublimity in the Novels of Ann Radcliffe: A Study of the Influence upon her Craft of Edmund Burke's* Enquiry into the Origin of our Ideas of the Sublime and Beautiful (Copenhagen: Ejnar Munksgaard, 1963).

> lime, that far from being produced by them, it anticipates our reasonings, and hurries us on by an irresistible force. (95-96)

The impact of Burke's theorizing, with its privileging of the powerful emotions of horror and terror, was immense: according to Samuel Holt Monk, Burke was

> responsible for much of the popularity of terror during the last half of the [eighteenth] century. No idea that became attached to the sublime failed to become popular. Terror enjoyed almost half a century of prominence, thanks to Burke, and out of the conviction that terror is sublime, came some, though not all, of the impulse that brought into existence the tale of terror.[1]

While Burke's theory was largely unconcerned with moral content—a fact which generated some opposition to Burke's aesthetic almost as soon as his work was published—it nonetheless struck a chord with late eighteenth century readers, who read and wrote novels of terror in increasing numbers, novels often scripted according to Burke's extensive catalog of those things which produce sublimity. From storms and cataracts to darkness, immense size, and obscurity, Burke's treatise ranged through a world of empirical experiences as it sought to map out human emotional responses. In an age already fascinated with aesthetics—owing, surely, to the fact aesthetics was often deeply interested in human psychology—Burke's potent theory provided a convenient formulary from which all manner of emotionally charged intoxicants could be retrieved, providing writers and readers with the tools they needed to chart the terrain of the mind.

Radcliffe's use of Burke (and those influenced by Burke, such as Joseph Priestley and the painter William Gilpin, who in turn influenced Charlotte Smith, one of Radcliffe's direct influences) is both frequent and assured, amply demonstrating her familiarity with Burke's theories and her growing mastery of literary technique. Whether by her frequent use of the word or by her repeated recourse to the Burkean catalog of sublime attributes, Radcliffe appropriates for her novel the allure and cachet of one of the eighteenth centu-

---

[1] Monk, *The Sublime: A Study of Critical Theories in XVIII-Century England* (New York: MLA, 1935): 218.

ry's hottest cultural topics while effectively using it to develop her characters and to locate them unambiguously on a moral and intellectual spectrum. The sublime, as a concept blending aesthetics and psychology—it is, after all, not just what one sees (Radcliffe actually described the impressions made by landscapes rather than their details, after all) but how one's careful and informed perception leads to particular intellectual and emotional responses—functions as a perfect barometer not only of an individual's state of moral and intellectual stature at any moment, but as a sort of testing ground: Emily's appropriate responses, even early in the novel, to sublime landscapes show that she is already sufficiently cultivated; her challenge becomes to maintain the appropriate pitch of that cultivation, to keep its informing sensibility in check as she encounters various "horrors" and threats in her journey to Udolpho and back.

Appendix F: Ann Radcliffe, "On the Supernatural in Poetry"

[The following discussion of the literary use of terror, and of its distinction from horror, was intended by Radcliffe to be part of the prologue to her novel *Gaston de Blondeville*, which was never published during her lifetime.[1] This prologue, from which the excerpt below is taken, appeared in *New Monthly Magazine*, volume 16 (1826), pp. 145-152. Radcliffe explains her theory and practice via the time-honored device of a fictional dialogue, in this case between two travelling companions, Mr. S— and Mr. W— (who will become Mr. Simpson and Mr. Willoughton in the frame of *Gaston de Blondeville*). Radcliffe is deeply indebted, in both this essay and in her novelistic renderings of terror experience, to Anna Lætitia Barbauld's essay "On the Pleasure Derived from Objects of Terror" (1773), with its illustrative fragment "Sir Bertrand" (long ascribed to Barbauld but actually written by her brother John Aikin).]

One of our travellers began a grave dissertation on the illusions of the imagination. "And not only on frivolous occasions," said he, "but in the most important pursuits of life, an object often flatters and charms at a distance, which vanishes into nothing as we approach it; and 'tis well if it leave only disappointment in our hearts. Sometimes a severer monitor is left there."

These truisms, delivered with an air of discovery by Mr. S—, who seldom troubled himself to think upon any subject, except that of a good dinner, were lost upon his companion, who, pursuing the airy conjectures which the present scene, however humbled, had called up, was following Shakspeare into unknown regions. "Where is now the undying spirit," said he, "that could so exquisitely perceive and feel? that could inspire itself with the various characters of this world, and create worlds of its own; to which the grand and the beautiful, the gloomy and the sublime of visible Nature, up-called not only corresponding feelings, but passions; which seemed to perceive a soul in every thing: and thus, in the secret workings of its own characters, and in the combinations of its incidents, kept the elements and local scenery always in unison with them, heightening

[1] The first modern edition of *Gaston de Blondeville* was recently published by Valancourt Books, with an introduction and notes by Frances Chiu.

their effect. So the conspirators at Rome[1] pass under the fiery showers and sheeted lightning of the thunder-storm, to meet, at midnight, in the porch of Pompey's theatre. The streets being then deserted by the affrighted multitude, that place, open as it was, was convenient for their council; and, as to the storm, they felt it not; it was not more terrible to them than their own passions, nor so terrible to others as the dauntless spirit that makes them, almost unconsciously, brave its fury. These appalling circumstances, with others of supernatural import, attended the fall of the conqueror of the world—a man, whose power Cassius represents to be dreadful as this night, when the sheeted dead were seen in the lightning to glide along the streets of Rome. How much does the sublimity of these attendant circumstances heighten our idea of the power of Caesar, of the terrific grandeur of his character, and prepare and interest us for his fate. The whole soul is roused and fixed, in the full energy of attention, upon the progress of the conspiracy against him; and, had not Shakspeare wisely withdrawn him from our view, there would have been no balance of our passions."—"Caesar was a tyrant," said Mr. S—. W— looked at him for a moment, and smiled, and then silently resumed the course of his own thoughts. No master ever knew how to touch the accordant springs of sympathy by small circumstances like our own Shakspeare. . . . Macbeth shows, by many instances, how much Shakspeare delighted to heighten the effect of his characters and his story by correspondent scenery: there the desolate heath, the troubled elements, assist the mischief of his malignant beings. But who, after hearing Macbeth's thrilling question—

— What are these,
So withered and so wild in their attire,
That look not like the inhabitants o' the earth,
And yet are on't?[2]

who would have thought of reducing them to mere human beings,

[1] Radcliffe is alluding to several scenes from Shakespeare's *Julius Caesar*, which follows the machinations of the men who conspire to assassinate the Roman emperor; the play makes powerful use of what would be, by Radcliffe's time, "gothic" conventions: storms, ghosts, gloom, etc.

[2] From Shakespeare's *Macbeth*, Act I, scene 3, lines 37-40; Banquo is referring in these lines to the witches, prominent minor characters in the play, who foretell, in riddling form, Macbeth's fortunes and fate as he seeks power for himself.

by attiring them not only like the inhabitants of the earth, but in the dress of a particular country, and making them downright Scotchwomen? thus not only contradicting the very words of Macbeth, but withdrawing from these cruel agents of the passions all that strange and supernatural air which had made them so affecting to the imagination, and which was entirely suitable to the solemn and important events they were foretelling and accomplishing. Another *improvement* on Shakspeare is the introducing a crowd of witches thus arrayed, instead of the three beings 'so withered and so wild in their attire.'

About the latter part of this sentence, W—, as he was apt to do, thought aloud, and Mr. S— said, "*I*, now, have sometimes considered, that it was quite sensible to make Scotch witches on the stage, appear like Scotch women. You must recollect that, in the superstition concerning witches, they lived familiarly upon the earth, mortal sorcerers, and were not always known from mere old women; consequently they must have appeared in the dress of the country where they happened to live, or they would have been more than suspected of witchcraft, which we find was not always the case."

"You are speaking of old women, and not of witches," said W— laughing, "and I must more than suspect you of crediting that obsolete superstition which destroyed so many wretched, yet guiltless persons, if I allow your argument to have any force. I am speaking of the only real witch—the witch of the poet; and all our notions and feelings connected with terror accord with his. The wild attire, the look *not of this earth*, are essential traits of supernatural agents, working evil in the darkness of mystery. Whenever the poet's witch condescends, according to the vulgar notion, to mingle mere ordinary mischief with her malignity, and to become familiar, she is ludicrous, and loses her power over the imagination; the illusion vanishes. So vexatious is the effect of the stage-witches upon my mind, that I should probably have left the theatre when they appeared, had not the fascination of Mrs. Siddons's[1] influence so spread itself over the whole play, as to overcome my disgust, and to make me forget even Shakspeare himself; while all consciousness of fiction was lost, and his thoughts lived and breathed before me in the very form of truth. . . ."

"I still think," said Mr. S—, without attending to these remarks,

---

[1] Sarah Siddons (1755-1831) was one of the most highly acclaimed actresses of her time.

"that, in a popular superstition, it is right to go with the popular notions, and dress your witches like the old women of the place where they are supposed to have appeared."

"As far as these notions prepare us for the awe which the poet designs to excite, I agree with you that he is right in availing himself of them; but, for this purpose, every thing familiar and common should be carefully avoided. In nothing has Shakspeare been more successful than in this; and in another case somewhat more difficult—that of selecting circumstances of manners and appearance for his supernatural beings, which, though wild and remote, in the highest degree, from common apprehension, never shock the understanding by incompatibility with themselves—never compel us, for an instant, to recollect that he has a licence for extravagance. Above every ideal being is the ghost of Hamlet, with all its attendant incidents of time and place. The dark watch upon the remote platform, the dreary aspect of the night, the very expression of the office on guard, 'the air bites shrewdly; it is very cold;'[1] the recollection of a star, an unknown world, are all circumstances which excite forlorn, melancholy, and solemn feelings, and dispose us to welcome, with trembling curiosity, the awful being that draws near; and to indulge in that strange mixture of horror, pity, and indignation, produced by the tale it reveals. Every minute circumstance of the scene between those watching on the platform, and of that between them and Horatio, preceding the entrance of the apparition, contributes to excite some feeling of dreariness, or melancholy, or solemnity, or expectation, in unison with, and leading on toward that high curiosity and thrilling awe with which we witness the conclusion of the scene. . . .

"Certainly you must be very superstitious," said Mr. S—, "or such things could not interest you thus."

"There are few people less so than I am," replied W—, "or I understand myself and the meaning of superstition very ill."

"That is quite paradoxical."

"It appears so, but so it is not. If I cannot explain this, take it as a mystery of the human mind."

"If it were possible for me to believe the appearance of ghosts at all," replied Mr. S—, "it would certainly be the ghost of Hamlet; but I never can suppose such things; they are out of all reason and probability."

---

[1] Act I, scene 4, line 1 in *Hamlet*, spoken by Hamlet himself shortly before he meets the ghost of his father.

"You would believe the immortality of the soul," said W—, with solemnity, "even without the aid of revelation; yet our confined faculties cannot comprehend *how* the soul may exist after separation from the body. I do not absolutely know that spirits are permitted to become visible to us on earth; yet that they may be permitted to appear for very rare and important purposes, such as could scarcely have been accomplished without an equal suspension, or a momentary change, of the laws prescribed to what we call *Nature*—that is, without one more exercise of the same creative power of which we must acknowledge so many millions of existing instances, and by which alone we ourselves at this moment breathe, think, or disquisite[1] at all, cannot be impossible, and, I think, is probable. Now, probability is enough for the poet's justification, the ghost being supposed to have come for an important purpose. Oh, I should never be weary of dwelling on the perfection of Shakspeare, in his management of every scene connected with that most solemn and mysterious being, which takes such entire possession of the imagination, that we hardly seem conscious we are beings of this world while we contemplate 'the extravagant and erring spirit.'[2] The spectre departs, accompanied by natural circumstances as touching as those with which he had approached. It is by the strange light of the glow-worm, which ''gins to pale his ineffectual fire';[3] it is at the first scent of the morning air—the living breath, that the apparition retires. There is, however, no little vexation in seeing the ghost of Hamlet *played*. The finest imagination is requisite to give the due colouring to such a character on the stage; and yet almost any actor is thought capable of performing it. In the scene where Horatio breaks his secret to Hamlet, Shakspeare, still true to the touch of circumstances, makes the time evening, and marks it by the very words of Hamlet, 'Good even, sir,' which Hanmer and Warburton changed, without any reason, to 'good morning,'[4] thus making Horatio relate his most interesting and solemn story by the clear light of the cheerfullest part of the day; when busy sounds are stirring, and the sun itself seems to contradict

---

[1] That is, to make a disquisition, to conduct a rational and systematic examination of a subject.

[2] *Hamlet* Act I, scene 1, line 135.

[3] *Hamlet* Act I, scene 5, line 90.

[4] Sir Thomas Hanmer and the Rev. William Warburton each produced important editions of Shakespeare's plays in 1744 and 1747, respectively.

every doubtful tale, and lessen every feeling of terror. The discord of this must immediately be understood by those who have bowed the willing soul to the poet."

"How happens it then," said Mr. S—, "that objects of terror sometimes strike us very forcibly, when introduced into scenes of gaiety and splendour, as, for instance, in the Banquet scene in Macbeth?"

"They strike, then, chiefly by the force of contrast," said W—; "but the effect, though sudden and strong, is also transient; it is the thrill of horror and surprise, which they then communicate, rather than the deep and solemn feelings excited under more accordant circumstances, and left long upon the mind. Who ever suffered for the ghost of Banquo, the gloomy and sublime kind of terror, which that of Hamlet calls forth? though the appearance of Banquo, at the high festival of Macbeth, not only tells us that he is murdered, but recalls to our minds the fate of the gracious Duncan, laid in silence and death by those who, in this very scene, are revelling in his spoils. There, though deep pity mingles with our surprise and horror, we experience a far less degree of interest, and that interest too of an inferior kind. The union of grandeur and obscurity, which Mr. Burke[1] describes as a sort of tranquillity tinged with terror, and which causes the sublime, is to be found only in Hamlet; or in scenes where circumstances of the same kind prevail."

"That may be," said Mr. S—, "and I perceive you are not one of those who contend that obscurity does not make any part of the sublime." "They must be men of very cold imaginations," said W—, "with whom certainty is more terrible than surmise. Terror and horror are so far opposite, that the first expands the soul, and awakens the faculties to a high degree of life; the other contracts, freezes, and nearly annihilates them. I apprehend, that neither Shakspeare nor Milton by their fictions, nor Mr. Burke by his reasoning, anywhere looked to positive horror as a source of the sublime, though they all agree that terror is a very high one; and where lies the great difference between horror and terror, but in the uncertainty and obscurity, that accompany the first, respecting the dreaded evil?"

"But what say you to Milton's image—'On his brow sat horror plumed.'"[2]

"As an image, it certainly is sublime; it fills the mind with an idea of power, but it does not follow that Milton intended to declare the feeling of horror to be sublime; and after all, his image imparts more of

---

[1] For Edmund Burke, see Appendix E.

[2] A slight misquotation from Book 4 of John Milton's *Paradise Lost*.

terror than of horror; for it is not distinctly pictured forth, but is seen in glimpses through obscuring shades, the great outlines only appearing, which excite the imagination to complete the rest; he only says, 'sat horror plumed'; you will observe, that the look of horror and the other characteristics are left to the imagination of the reader; and according to the strength of that, he will feel Milton's image to be either sublime or otherwise. Milton, when he sketched it, probably felt, that not even his art could fill up the outline, and present to other eyes the countenance which his "mind's eye" gave to him. Now, if obscurity has so much effect on fiction, what must it have in real life, when to ascertain the object of our terror, is frequently to acquire the means of escaping it. You will observe, that this image, though indistinct or obscure, is not confused."

"How can any thing be indistinct and not confused?" said Mr. S—.

"Ay, that question is from the new school," replied W—; "but recollect, that obscurity, or indistinctness, is only a negative, which leaves the imagination to act upon the few hints that truth reveals to it; confusion is a thing as positive as distinctness, though not necessarily so palpable; and it may, by mingling and confounding one image with another, absolutely counteract the imagination, instead of exciting it. Obscurity leaves something for the imagination to exaggerate; confusion, by blurring one image into another, leaves only a chaos in which the mind can find nothing to be magnificent, nothing to nourish its fears or doubts, or to act upon in any way; yet confusion and obscurity are terms used indiscriminately by those, who would prove, that Shakspeare and Milton were wrong when they employed obscurity as a cause of the sublime, that Mr. Burke was equally mistaken in his reasoning upon the subject, and that mankind have been equally in error, as to the nature of their own feelings, when they were acted upon by the illusions of those great masters of the imagination, at whose so potent bidding, the passions have been awakened from their sleep, and by whose magic a crowded Theatre has been changed to a lonely shore, to a witch's cave, to an enchanted island, to a murderer's castle, to the ramparts of an usurper, to the battle, to the midnight carousal of the camp or the tavern, to every various scene of the living world."

Printed in the United States
104788LV00001B/347/A

9 780977 784189